Bunnicula

Bunnicula

A Rabbit-Tale of Mystery

by DEBORAH and JAMES HOWE

ILLUSTRATED BY ALAN DANIEL

Atheneum Books for Young Readers

Atheneum Books for Young Readers
An imprint of Simon & Schuster Children's Publishing Division
1230 Avenue of the Americas
New York, New York 10020

Revised format edition, 1999

Printed in the United States of America

10 9 8 7 6 5 4 3 2 1

Library of Congress Cataloging-in-Publication Data:
Howe, Deborah.
Bunnicula: a rabbit-tale of mystery / by Deborah and James Howe;
illustrated by Alan Daniel. –Rev. format ed.
p. cm.
Summary: This reissue of the classic story featuring the vampire
rabbit celebrates the book's twentieth anniversary. Includes an essay by
coauthor James Howe on the origins of "Bunnicula."
ISBN 0-689-83219-2
[1. Rabbits–Fiction. 2. Vampires–Fiction. 3. Mystery and detective stories.]
I. Howe, James, 1946-   II. Daniel, Alan, 1939- ill.   III. Title.
PZ7.H836Bu   1999   [Fic]–dc21   99-28790

To

MILDRED AND LESTER SMITH

—with love

Contents

We wish to thank

Lucy Kroll, Bernice Chardiet

and our editor, Jean Karl,

for their guidance and encouragement,

and to acknowledge

the love and support of our family

and friends.

THE BOOK you are about to read was brought to my attention in a most unusual way. One Friday afternoon, just before closing time, I heard a scratching sound at the front door of my office. When I opened the door, there before me stood a sad-eyed, droopy-eared dog carrying a large, plain envelope in his mouth. He dropped it at my feet, gave me a soulful glance and with great, quiet dignity sauntered away.

Inside the envelope was the manuscript of the book you now hold in your hands, together with this letter:

Gentlemen:

The enclosed story is true. It happened in this very town, to me and the family with whom I reside. I have changed the names of the family in order to protect them, but in all other respects, everything you will read here is factual.

Allow me to introduce myself. My name is

Harold. I come to writing purely by chance. My full-time occupation is dog. I live with Mr. and Mrs. X (called here the "Monroes") and their two sons: Toby, aged eight and Pete, aged ten. Also sharing our home is a cat named Chester, whom I am pleased to call my friend. We were a typical American family—and still are, though the events related in my story have, of course, had their effect on our lives.

I hope you will find this tale of sufficient interest to yourself and your readers to warrant its publication.

Sincerely,
Harold X.

Bunnicula

ONE

The Arrival

I SHALL never forget the first time I laid these now tired old eyes on our visitor. I had been left home by the family with the admonition to take care of the house until they returned. That's something they always say to me when they go out: "Take care of the house, Harold. You're the watchdog." I think it's their way of making up for not taking me with them. As if I *wanted* to go anyway. You can't lie down at the movies and still see the screen. And people think you're being impolite if you fall asleep and start to snore, or scratch yourself in public. No thank you, I'd rather be stretched out on my favorite rug in front of a nice, whistling radiator.

But I digress. I was talking about that first night. Well, it was cold, the rain was pelting the windows, the wind was howling, and it felt pretty good to be indoors. I was lying on the rug with my head on my paws just staring absently at the front door. My friend Chester was curled up on the brown velvet armchair, which years ago he'd staked out as his own. I saw that once again he'd covered the whole seat with his cat hair, and I chuckled to myself, picturing the scene tomorrow. (Next to grasshoppers, there is nothing that frightens Chester more than the vacuum cleaner.)

In the midst of this reverie, I heard a car pull into the driveway. I didn't even bother to get up and see who it was. I knew it had to be my family —the Monroes—since it was just about time for the movie to be over. After a moment, the front door flew open. There they stood in the doorway: Toby and Pete and Mom and Dad Monroe. There was a flash of lightning, and in its glare I noticed that Mr. Monroe was carrying a little bundle—a bundle with tiny glistening eyes.

Pete and Toby bounded into the room, both

talking at the top of their lungs. Toby shouted, "Put him over here, Dad."

"Take your boots off. You're soaking wet," replied his mother, somewhat calmly I thought, under the circumstances.

"But Mom, what about the—"

"First, stop dripping on the carpet."

"Would somebody like to take this?" asked Mr. Monroe, indicating the bundle with the eyes. "I'd like to remove my coat."

"I will," Pete yelled.

"No, I will," said Toby "I found him."

"You'll drop him."

"I will not."

"You will too."

"Mom, Pete punched me!"

"*I'll* take him," said Mrs. Monroe. "Take off your coats this minute!" But she became so involved in helping the boys out of their coats that she didn't take him at all.

My tranquil evening had been destroyed and no one had even said hello to me. I whimpered to remind them that I was there.

"Harold!" cried Toby, "guess what happened

to me." And then, all over again, everyone started talking at once.

At this point, I feel I must explain something. In our family, everyone treats everyone else with great respect for his or her intelligence. That goes for the animals as well as the people. Everything that happens to them is explained to us. It's never been just "Good boy, Harold," or "Use the litter box, Chester" at our house. Oh no, with us it's "Hey Harold, Dad got a raise and now we're in a higher tax bracket," or "Come sit on the bed, Chester, and watch this *Wild Kingdom* show. Maybe you'll see a relative." Which shows just how thoughtful they are. But after all, Mr. Monroe *is* a college professor and Mrs. Monroe *is* a lawyer, so we think of it as a rather special household. And we are, therefore, rather special pets. So it wasn't at all surprising to me that they took the time to explain the strange circumstances surrounding the arrival of the little bundle with the glistening eyes now among us.

It seems that they had arrived at the theater late, and rather than trip over the feet of the audience already seated, they decided to sit in the last row, which was empty. They tiptoed in and sat down very quietly, so they wouldn't disturb anyone. Suddenly, Toby, who's the little one, sprang up from his chair and squealed that he had sat on something. Mr. Monroe told him to stop making a fuss and move to another seat, but in an unusual display of independence, Toby said he wanted to see just what it was he had sat on. An usher came over to their row to shush them, and Mr. Monroe borrowed his flashlight. What they found on Toby's chair was the little blanketed bundle that was now sitting on Mr. Monroe's lap.

They now unwrapped the blanket, and there in the center was a tiny black and white rabbit, sitting in a shoebox filled with dirt. A piece of paper had been tied to his neck with a ribbon. There were words on the paper, but the Monroes were unable to decipher them because they were in a totally unfamiliar language. I moved closer for a better look.

Now, most people might call me a mongrel, but I have some pretty fancy bloodlines running through these veins and Russian wolfhound happens to be one of them. Because my family got around a lot, I was able to recognize the language as an obscure dialect of the Carpathian Mountain region. Roughly translated, it read, "Take good care of my baby." But I couldn't tell if it was a note from a bereaved mother or a piece of Roumanian sheet music.

The little guy was shivering from fear and cold. It was decided that Mr. Monroe and the boys would make a house for him out of an old crate and some heavy-duty wire mesh from the garage. For the night, the boys would make a bed for him in the shoebox. Toby and Pete ran outside to find the crate, and Mrs. Monroe went to the kitchen to get him some milk and lettuce. Mr. Monroe sat down, a dazed expression in his eyes, as if he were wondering how he came to be sitting in his own living room in a wet raincoat with a strange bunny on his lap.

I signaled to Chester and the two of us casually moseyed over to a corner of the room. We looked at each other.

"Well, what do you think?" I asked.

"I don't think rabbits like milk," he answered.

CHESTER and I were unable to continue our conversation because a deafening crash commanded our attention.

Pete yelled from the hallway: "Maaa! Toby broke the rabbit's house!"

"I didn't, I just dropped it. Pete won't let me carry it."

"It's too big. Toby's too little."

"I am not!"

"You are too!"

"Okay, fellas," Mrs. Monroe called out as she entered with the milk and lettuce. "Let's try to get it in here with as little hysteria as possible, please."

Chester turned to me and said under his breath, "That lettuce looks repulsive, but if there's any milk left, *I* get it." I certainly wasn't going to argue with him. I'm a water man myself.

At that moment, the crate arrived, barely standing the strain of being pulled in two directions at once.

The Arrival

"Ma, Toby says he's going to keep the rabbit in his room. That's not fair. Harold sleeps in his room."

Only sometimes, I thought, when I know he's got a leftover ham sandwich in his drawer. Toby's a nice kid, don't get me wrong, but it doesn't hurt that he shares his stash with me. It was, after all, at one of those late night parties in Toby's room that I first developed my taste for chocolate cake. And Toby, noting my preference, has kept me in chocolate cake ever since. Pete, on the other hand, doesn't believe in sharing. And the only time I tried to sleep on his bed, he rolled over on me and pinned me by my ears so that I couldn't move for the rest of the night. I had a crick in my neck for days.

"But he's mine," Toby said. "I found him."

"You sat on him, you mean!"

"I found him, and he's sleeping in my room."

"You can keep smelly ol' Harold in your room, and Chester too, if you want to, but I'm going to keep the rabbit in mine."

Smelly ol' Harold! I would have bitten his ankle, but I knew he hadn't changed his socks for a week. Smelly, indeed!

Mr. Monroe spoke up. "I think the best place for the rabbit is right here in the living room on that table by the window. It's light there, and he'll get lots of fresh air."

"Pete's taller than I am," Toby cried. "He'll be able to see the rabbit better."

"Too bad, squirt."

"Okay," said Mrs. Monroe through clenched teeth, "let's put him to bed and make him comfortable, and then we can all get some sleep."

"Why?" Pete asked. "I don't want to go to sleep."

Mrs. Monroe smiled a little too sweetly at Pete.

"Look, Ma," said Toby, "he's not drinking his milk."

Chester nudged me in the ribs. "Didn't I tell you?" he asked. "Excuse me while I make myself available."

"Hey," said Toby, "we gotta name him."

"Can't that wait until tomorrow?" asked Mr. Monroe.

The boys shouted in unison: "No! He has to have a name right now." I have to say I agreed

with them. It took them three days to name me,
and those were the three most anxious days of
my life. I couldn't sleep at all, worrying that they
were really going to call me Fluffy as Mrs. Monroe had suggested.

"Well, all right," sighed Mrs. Monroe, "what
about . . . oh, say . . . Bun-Bun?"

Oh, oh. There she goes again, I thought. Where
does she get them?

"Yech!" we all said.

"Well, then, how about Fluffy?" she offered
hopefully.

Pete looked at his mother and smiled. "You
never give up, do you, Ma?"

Meanwhile, Chester (who had also been named
Fluffy for a short time) was rubbing against Mrs.
Monroe's ankles and purring loudly.

"No, Chester, not now," she said, pushing him
aside.

"He wants to help us name him, don't you
Chester?" Toby asked, as he scooped him up into
his arms. Chester shot me a look. I could tell this
was not what he had in mind.

"Come on, Harold," Toby called, "you've got

to help with the name, too."

I joined the family and serious thinking began. We all peered into the box. It was the first time I had really seen him. So, this is a rabbit, I thought. He sort of looks like Chester, only he's got longer ears and a shorter tail. And a motor in his nose.

"Well," said Pete, after a moment, "since we found him at the movies, why don't we call him Mr. Johnson?"

There was a moment of silence.

"Who's Mr. Johnson?" asked Toby.

"The guy who owns the movie theater," Pete answered.

No one seemed to like the idea.

"How about Prince?" said Mr. Monroe.

"Dad," said Toby, "are you kidding?"

"Well, I had a dog named Prince once," he replied lamely.

Prince, I thought, that's a silly name for a dog.

"We found him at a Dracula movie. Let's call him Dracula," Toby said.

"That's a stupid name," said Pete.

"No, it's not! And anyway, I found him, so I should get to name him."

The Arrival

"Mom, you're not going to let him name him, are you? That's favoritism, and I'll be traumatized if you do."

Mrs. Monroe looked in wonder at Pete.

"Please Mom, please Dad, let's name him Dracula," cried Toby, "please, please, please." And with each *please,* he squeezed Chester a little harder.

Mrs. Monroe picked up the bowl of milk and moved toward the kitchen. Chester followed her every movement with his eyes, which now seemed to be popping out of his head. When she reached the kitchen door, she turned back and said, "Let's not have any more arguments. We'll compromise. He's a bunny and we found him at a Dracula movie, so we'll call him Bunny-cula. Bun*nic*ula! That should make everybody happy, including me."

"What about me?" muttered Chester. "I won't be happy until she puts down that milk."

"Well, guys, is that okay with you?" she asked.

Toby and Pete looked at one another. And then at the rabbit. A smile grew on Toby's face.

"Yeah, Ma, I think that name is just right."

Pete shrugged. "It's okay. But I get to feed him."

"Okay, I'm going to put the milk back in the fridge. Maybe he'll drink it tomorrow."

"What about Chester?" Toby said, dropping the frantic cat to the floor. "Maybe he would like it." Chester made a beeline for Mrs. Monroe and looked up at her plaintively.

"Oh, Chester doesn't want any more milk, do you, Chester? You've already had your milk today." She reached down, patted Chester on his head and walked into the kitchen. Chester didn't move.

"Okay, bedtime," said Mr. Monroe.

"Good night, Bunnicula," Toby said.

"Good night, Count Bunnicula," Pete said sarcastically, in what I took to be his attempt at a Transylvanian accent. I may be wrong but I thought I saw a flicker of movement from the cage.

"Good night, Harold. Good night, Chester." I licked Toby good night.

"Good night, smelly Harold. Good night, dumb Chester." I drooled on Pete's foot. "Mom,

Harold drooled on my foot!"

"GOODNIGHT, PETE!" Mrs. Monroe said with great finality as she came back into the living room, and then more calmly, "Good night, Harold. Good night, Chester."

Mr. and Mrs. Monroe went up the stairs together.

"You know, dear," Mr. Monroe said, "that was very clever. Bunnicula. I could never have thought of a name like that."

"Oh, I don't know, Robert." She smiled, as she put her arm through his. "I think Prince is a lovely name, too."

The room was quiet. Chester was still sitting by the closed kitchen door in a state of shock. Slowly, he turned to me.

"I wish they *had* named him Fluffy," was all he said.

TWO

Music
in the Night

I FEEL at this time there are a few things you should know about Chester. He is not your ordinary cat. (But then, I'm not your ordinary dog, since an ordinary dog wouldn't be writing this book, would he?)

Chester came into the house several years ago as a birthday gift for Mr. Monroe, along with two volumes of G. K. Chesterton (hence the name, Chester) and a first edition of Dickens' *A Tale of Two Cities*. As a result of this introduction to literature, and given the fact that Mr. Monroe is an English professor, Chester developed a taste for reading early in life. (I, on the other hand, have developed a taste for books. I found *Jonathan Livingston Seagull* particularly delicious.) From Chester's kittenhood on, Mr. Monroe has used him as a sounding board for all his student lectures. If Chester doesn't fall asleep when Mr. Monroe is talking, the lecture can be counted a success.

Every night when the family is sleeping, Chester goes to the bookshelf, selects his midnight reading and curls up on his favorite chair. He especially likes mystery stories and tales of horror and the supernatural. As a result, he has developed a very vivid imagination.

I'm telling you this, because I think it's important for you to know something of Chester's background before I relate to you the story of the events following the arrival of Bunnicula into our home. Let me begin with that first night.

It seems that after I went to sleep, Chester, still stewing over the lost milk, settled down with his latest book and attempted to ignore the rumbling in his stomach. The room was dark and quiet. This did not prevent his reading, of course, since as you know, cats can see in the dark. A shaft of moonlight fell across the rabbit's cage and spilled onto the floor below. The wind and rain had stopped and, as Chester read Edgar Allan Poe's "The Fall of the House of Usher," he became increasingly aware of the eerie stillness that had taken their place. As Chester tells it, he suddenly felt compelled to look at the rabbit.

"I don't know what came over me," he said to me the next morning, "but a cold chill ran down my spine."

The little bunny had begun to move for the first time since he had been put in his cage. He lifted his tiny nose and inhaled deeply, as if gathering sustenance from the moonlight.

"He slicked his ears back close to his body, and for the first time," Chester said, "I noticed the peculiar marking on his forehead. What had seemed an ordinary black spot between his ears took on a strange v-shape, which connected with the big black patch that covered his back and each side of his neck. It looked as if he was wearing a coat . . . no, more like a *cape* than a coat."

Through the silence had drifted the strains of

a remote and exotic music.

"I could have sworn it was a gypsy violin," Chester told me. "I thought perhaps a caravan was passing by, so I ran to the window."

I remembered my mother telling me something about caravans when I was a puppy. But for the life of me, I couldn't remember what.

"What's a caravan?" I asked, feeling a little stupid.

"A caravan is a band of gypsies traveling through the forest in their wagons," Chester answered.

"Ah, yes." It was coming back to me now. "Station wagons?"

"No, covered wagons! The gypsies travel all through the land, setting up camps around great bonfires, doing magical tricks, and sometimes, if you cross their palms with a piece of silver, they'll tell your fortune."

"You mean if I gave them a fork, they'd tell my fortune?" I asked, breathlessly.

Chester looked at me with disdain. "Save your silverware," he said, "it wasn't a caravan after all."

I was disappointed. "What was it?" I asked.

Chester explained that when he looked out the window, he saw Professor Mickelwhite, our next door neighbor, playing the violin in his living room. He listened for a few moments to the haunting melody and sighed with relief. I've really got to stop reading these horror stories late at night, he thought, it's beginning to affect my mind. He yawned and turned to go back to his chair and get some sleep. As he turned, however, he was startled by what he saw.

There in the moonlight, as the music filtered through the air, sat the bunny, his eyes intense and staring, an unearthly aura about them.

"Now, this is the part you won't believe," Chester said to me, "but as I watched, his lips parted in a hideous smile, and where a rabbit's buck teeth should have been, two little pointed fangs glistened."

I wasn't sure what to make of Chester's story, but the way he told it, it set my hair on end.

[THREE]

Some Unusual
Goings-On

THE next few days passed uneventfully. I was very bored. Our new arrival slept all day, and Chester, whose curiosity had been aroused by the strange behavior of the rabbit that first night, had decided to stay awake every night to observe him. Therefore, he too spent most of his days sleeping. So *I* had no one to talk to.

The evenings weren't much better. Toby and Pete, who used to play with me as soon as they got home from school, now ran immediately to that silly rabbit's cage to play with him. Or at least they'd try to. Bunnicula did not make the most energetic playmate. It took him quite a while to wake up each night and then when he did awaken, he didn't do much except hop around the living room. He didn't play catch, he didn't fetch, he didn't roll over to get his tummy rubbed. I couldn't understand why they played with him at all. I expect it was because he was new and different. But I was confident that they would soon tire of him and come back to trusty ol' Harold.

Finally, on the morning of the fourth day, I caught Chester bleary-eyed over the water dish. He grumbled at me in a most unpleasant manner.

"You know, Chester, you were never exactly charming in the morning, but lately you've become downright grumpy."

Chester growled in response.

"What are you doing this for anyway? What are you looking for? He's just a cute little bunny."

"Cute little bunny!" Chester was amazed at my character analysis. "That's what you think. He's a danger to this household and everyone in it."

"Oh, Chester," I said, with an indulgent smile, "I think your reading has gone to your head."

"It's just because I do read that I know what I'm talking about."

"Well, what are you talking about? I still don't understand."

"I'm not sure yet, but I know there's something funny about that rabbit. That's why I have to keep alert."

"But look at you—you're exhausted. You sleep all the time. How can you call that alert?"

"I'm awake when it's important. He sleeps all day, so I sleep all day."

"So just what have you seen since that first night that makes you uneasy?"

"Well . . ." said Chester, "I, uh . . . that is . . ." At this point, Chester started to bathe his tail, which is a cat's way of changing a subject he finds uncomfortable. He then stumbled sleepily into the living room.

"So?" I asked again, following him, "what have you seen?"

"Nothing!" he snapped, and proceeded to curl up on his chair to go to sleep. After a moment, he opened one eye. "But that doesn't mean there's nothing *to* see."

Some Unusual Goings-On

For the next few mornings, it was the same routine. I'd be ready for a good romp around the living room, and Chester would go to sleep. Pete and Toby were at school. Mr. Monroe was at the university (he never did too much romping around, anyway). And Mrs. Monroe was at her office.

No one to play with poor, neglected Harold. At first, I thought I could strike up a friendship with Bunnicula and maybe teach him a few tricks. But I could never wake him up. He was always waking up just about sunset, when I wanted to take a snooze. A rabbit, I concluded, is cute to look at, but is generally useless, especially as a companion to dogs. So, I would retire each day with my favorite shoe to the rug and chew.

Now, some people (especially Mr. and Mrs. Monroe) can't understand my taste for shoes and yell at me for snacking on them. But I always say there's no accounting for taste. For instance, I remember one evening when Mr. Monroe picked some of his sour balls out of the bowl by his chair and dropped a green one on the floor. He didn't notice as it rolled across the room and landed near my nose. I decided this was a perfect opportunity to try one for myself. I placed it in my mouth . . . and wished immediately that I hadn't. As the tears started running out of my eyes, I thought, What's wrong with my mouth?! It's turning inside out!

Mr. Monroe immediately noticed that something had happened. "What's the matter, Harold? Are you looking for someone to kiss?"

"Help! Help!" I wanted to cry, but all that came out was an *"ooooo"* sound. I *"ooooo"*-ed for days.

So how can anyone who likes green sourballs criticize me for preferring a nice penny loafer or a bedroom slipper?

But back to the matter at hand:

One morning, Chester had news.

"That bunny," he whispered to me across our food bowls, "got out of his cage last night."

"Don't be ridiculous," I said. "How could he break through that wire? Look how little he is."

"That's just it! He didn't break through any wire. He got out of his cage without breaking anything, or opening any doors!"

I looked puzzled. So Chester told me the following story.

"Now, Harold," he said, "I don't want you thinking I'm not a good watchcat, but after a few hours last night, I grew curious about the time. I went into the hallway and . . . you know that new clock they've got? The big one? That goes all the way to the ceiling? Well, see, it has this thing in the middle called a pendulum. At first, I figured I would just leave it alone. It looked like that spool they tied on a string and hung from the doorknob for me to play with when I was a kitten. Everytime I hit that silly spool with my paw, it would swing back and hit me on the nose. I hated that toy. So naturally, when I saw this one, I decided not to have anything to do with it. I checked the time. It was midnight. I was all set to go back to the living room when something stopped me."

"Curiosity?" I ventured.

"I suppose you could call it that. I prefer to think of it as the challenge of the unknown. I put one paw over my nose and reached out with the other one and gave it one good smack. I darn near broke my arm. It's still tender; see how swollen it is."

He showed me his little paw. I couldn't see anything wrong. But I knew better than to argue with him. "Oh yes," I said, "that looks terrible. You must be suffering awfully. You'd better go easy today." He limped dramatically, just far enough to display his new handicap, and continued.

"I couldn't even get to the pendulum. Somebody had put glass in front of it, and I was pretty mad. I was all set to go back, but at the same time, I couldn't help watching the thing move back and forth, back and forth. Back and forth . . . It was so easy to watch, and before I knew what had happened, I was waking up."

"You fell asleep?" I asked incredulously.

"I couldn't help it. I didn't even know it had happened. But I looked up at the face of the clock and it was twelve forty-five! I'd been gone forty-five minutes. I ran back into the living room, looked at Bunnicula's cage, and it was empty. I couldn't imagine where he was. Then I noticed a light coming from under the kitchen door. I went into a crouch, stalking the light, when . . . *click* . . . I heard the refrigerator door close, and the light went out."

"It must have been Mr. Monroe having his midnight snack," I suggested.

"No, that's what I thought. I jumped on my chair, curled up real quick and kept one eye open, pretending to be asleep. Slowly, the door to the kitchen squeaked open. This little head poked out from around the corner and looked to either side to see if the coast was clear. Then . . . guess who came bouncing out all by himself, and with that idiotic grin of his plastered all over his face?"

"Well . . . I guess it wasn't Mr. Monroe," I said.

"Not unless he wears bunny pajamas and gets very tiny at night."

"Bunnicula, huh?"

"You got it. Unfortunately, I hadn't positioned myself so that I could see him get back into the cage. And I didn't want to let him know that I had seen anything, so I had to stay put. I still don't know how he got out, or back in."

At this point, Mr. Monroe came downstairs to make breakfast.

I wondered if Chester hadn't dreamed the whole thing. He did admit he'd fallen asleep and, as I've said, he has quite an imagination. But I was game. After all, there hadn't been any excitement in this place for days. Chester and I took our positions under the kitchen table. We didn't have long to wait.

"Holy cow!" Mr. Monroe yelped as he opened the refrigerator door. He took this funny-looking white thing out of the fridge and held it at arm's length.

"Peter, come down here!"

"What is that?" I whispered.

"Beats me," Chester answered. "It looks like a white tomato."

"Very funny," I said, as Pete came into the kitchen.

"Peter, have you been playing with your chemistry set in here?"

"No, Dad, why?"

"I thought this might be one of your experiments. Do you know what it is?"

"Gee, Dad, it looks like a white tomato."

Just then, Mrs. Monroe and Toby came in the door.

"What's all the fuss about?" Mrs. Monroe asked.

"We were just trying to figure out what this is."

Toby pulled it down so he could get a better look.

"Well," he said, "it looks to me like a white tomato."

Mr. Monroe took a good long look. "You know," he said to his wife, "it really does look like a white tomato."

"There's one way to find out," said Mrs. Monroe, who always was the practical one. "Let's cut it open and see what's inside."

Everybody gathered around the table. I jumped up on a chair, and in all the excitement, no one noticed that I had my paws on the table (which under normal circumstances was discouraged, to say the least). Chester wasn't so lucky.

"Chester, get off the table," Mrs. Monroe said. Chester jumped onto Toby's shoulders, where he stayed to view the proceedings.

Mrs. Monroe took her sharpest knife and cut cleanly through the thing. It fell into two halves.

"It's a tomato, all right," said Mrs. Monroe. "Here are the seeds."

"But it's all white," Toby observed.

"And look," said Pete, "it's dry."

"So it is," Mr. Monroe said, as he picked up one of the halves. "There is no juice at all. Well, Ann, what do you think?"

"It's gone bad, I guess, though I've never heard of a tomato turning white before. Come on," she said, clearing the table, "let's throw it out and have breakfast. And Harold, get your paws off the table."

Rats.

Chester jumped down from Toby's shoulders and motioned for me to follow him into the living room.

"This had better be important," I said. "They're cooking bacon."

"A white tomato. Very significant," Chester murmured.

"So it's a white tomato," I said, edging my way back to the kitchen door. "What does that have to do with Bunnicula?"

"I can tell you one thing," Chester said. "I got a good look at the tomato. There were very suspicious marks on the skin."

"So?"

"I believe they're teeth marks."

"So?"

"So tonight I'm going to reread a book I read last year."

"How fascinating," I said, as the aroma of frying bacon wafted across my nostrils. "And what book might that be?"

"*The Mark of the Vampire!*"

"What!" I stopped dead in my tracks.

"Meet me tonight after the others have gone to sleep. You'd better take a nap today so you can stay awake."

Chester closed his eyes. I shifted my look to Bunnicula, who seemed to be asleep in his cage. A tiny smile sat upon his lips. A happy dream? I wondered, or something else?

My reverie was broken by the sound of crunching bacon. I was in the kitchen in a flash.

$\mathcal{A}$ $\mathcal{C}at$ $\mathcal{P}repares$

I ALMOST didn't make it to my meeting with Chester that night. Toby had a feast in his room. It was Friday night, and on Friday nights, Toby gets to stay up and read as late as he wants to. So, of course, he needs lots of food to keep up his strength. Good food like cheese crackers, chocolate cupcakes (my very favorite, the kind with cream in the middle, *mmmm!*), pretzels and peanut butter sandwiches. The last I cannot abide because my mouth always gets stuck. Chocolate cupcakes with cream in the center, however, are another story.

This particular evening, I stationed myself on Toby's stomach. Usually, I'm a little more subtle but, having missed out on the bacon at breakfast, I was not about to take any chances on the chocolate cupcakes (with cream in the center).

Toby knew what I was after. But sometimes he thinks he's funny, and he plays little games with me.

"Hi, Harold, I'll bet you'd like a peanut butter sandwich, wouldn't you? Here, you have this one that's leftover from yesterday, while I eat this boring old chocolate cupcake—which is nice and fresh and has cream in the middle. Okay, Harold?"

Ha ha. My sides are splitting.

"What's the matter? Don't you want the peanut butter sandwich? All right, I'll put it away for another night. Oh, here's something you might like. It's a green sourball from Dad's candy dish that was stuck to my sock. Would you like that, huh, pal?"

Oh boy, the kid is really hot tonight.

"No, huh? Well, I'd give you one of my cupcakes, but I know how much you hate chocolate."

Would a little drooling on your stomach help convince you otherwise?

"Oh, you like chocolate! Okay then, you can have both of them!"

One thing I have to say about Toby: Although he's got a rotten sense of humor, he's a nice kid. Naturally, once I'd eaten both cupcakes (which took approximately four seconds), I felt obliged to hang around and let Toby know I was grateful. What better way than to share a few of his cheese crackers?

"Well, Harold," Toby said some time later, "we've had quite a party, but I have to go to sleep now. I can't keep my eyes open, so I'll have to wait until tomorrow to find out what happens in the next chapter. This is a good book, Harold. It's called *Treasure Island,* and it's by a man named Robert Louis Stevenson. It's kind of hard reading, though. I have to keep looking the big words up in the dictionary, so it's taking me a long time to get through it."

I've always had trouble with words myself. Half the time they don't mean what I think they're going to, and then, even when I do find out what they mean, I forget the next day anyway. You might say that I'm smart—but just not the scholarly type.

"But it's a really good story," Toby continued. "It's all about pirates and this little boy just like me."

No dogs?

"And a parrot, Harold."

A parrot? What's a parrot? Is there anything about chocolate cake? That's my idea of a treasure.

"Well, good night, Harold. If you're going to sleep here, you'll have to get off my stomach because it's a little full right now."

Good night, Toby.

I curled up at the foot of the bed, but I couldn't sleep trying to figure out what a parrot was. I thought it might be a lady pirate, since the words sounded something alike, but then again, I thought it might be an umbrella. Chester would know, I thought, so I went downstairs to ask him.

"WELL, you certainly took your time," Chester snapped as I sauntered casually into the room. "I finished my book half an hour ago. Where were you?"

"It so happens I was discussing great works of

literature with Toby."

"Since when is a Twinkies wrapper considered a great work of literature?"

I decided to ignore that. Unfortunately, several chocolate crumbs fell from my mouth to the floor at precisely that moment.

"As a matter of fact," I said, trying valiantly to regain my dignity, "we were talking about *Treasure Island*. Ever hear of it?"

"Ever hear of it?" he sneered. "I read *that* when I was a kitten."

"Oh. Then, tell me, Chester, what is a parrot?"

Chester looked at me scornfully. "A parrot," he said, "is a tropical zygodactyl bird (order psittaciformes) that has a stout curved hooked bill, is often crested, brightly variegated and an excellent mimic. In other words, Harold, a parrot is a little bird with a big mouth."

"Oh," I said after a moment. "I thought maybe it was an umbrella."

"Did you get so busy discussing parrots with Toby that you forgot you were going to meet me here? This is important, Harold."

I still wasn't sure what a parrot was, but I

decided this was not the time to pursue it.

"Come over here," Chester commanded, indicating his chair, "and let me show you this book."

I looked at the chair. Chester was already sitting in it, with a very large book open in front of him.

"I don't think there's going to be room for both of us, Chester," I said.

"Come on, come on, you're wasting time. Just jump up here."

I surveyed the scene carefully. I knew I would have to get a running start since there was just a tiny spot left for me and I would never be able to fit into it if I pulled myself up slowly. Apparently, I was taking too long for Chester's liking.

"Will you get up here?" he hissed.

Okay, if that's what you want. I ran and jumped onto the chair, landing with a great kerplop.

"Chester, where are you?" I cried. I couldn't see anything but the back of the chair. I'd forgotten to turn myself around.

"I'm here, you great oaf!"

I turned my head. "What are you doing on the floor?" I asked.

"You knocked me off the chair. Now just stay put. I'm coming back up."

I moved to the back of the chair, and Chester landed on the front.

"Now, let's see," he said, "we both have to see the book. You come over here, and I'll move this way."

I don't know if you've ever watched a cat try to decide where to sit, but it involves a lot of circling around, sitting, getting up again, circling some more, thinking about it, lying down, standing up, bathing a paw or tail and . . . circling! A dog, on the other hand, sits. "This looks like a good spot," a dog will say to himself. He will then lower his body to the spot in question and is usually so secure in his decision that he will fall asleep immediately.

Chester took what felt like twenty minutes to settle himself in, and just as I was drifting off, the kicks started. "Come on, Harold, quit hogging the seat. And wake up. What were you trying to do? Take a little cat nap? Ha ha ha."

I yawned.

"Now," said Chester, turning to the book, "let's get down to brass tacks."

"What exactly is on your mind?" I asked.

"This book and that rabbit," Chester replied. "Now tell me, Harold, have you noticed anything funny about that rabbit?"

"No," I said, "but I've certainly noticed a lot of funny things about you recently."

"Think about it. That rabbit sleeps all day."

"So do I. So do you."

"Furthermore, he's got funny little sharp teeth."

"So do I. So do you."

"Furthermore, he gets in and out of his cage by himself. What kind of rabbit can do that?"

"A smart one," I said. "I could do it."

"We're not talking about you, Harold. We're talking about the rabbit. Now, where did they find him?"

"At the movies."

"Yes, but *what* movie?"

"Dracula," I said, "so?"

"So," he said quickly, "remember the note around his neck? What language was it in?"

"An obscure dialect of the Carpathian mountain region," I answered smugly. He didn't know everything.

"Ah ha!" Chester said, "but what *area* of the Carpathian mountain region?"

Area? What's an area? I looked at him blankly.

"Transylvania!" he cried triumphantly. "And that proves my point."

"What point? What are we talking about?"

"And don't forget the white tomato! That's most important of all!"

"But, what . . ."

"This book," said Chester, disregarding me, "tells us just what we need to know."

"*What?*" I practically screamed. "What does it tell us? What does this book have to do with Bunnicula? What are you talking about? What's going on here? I can't stand it anymore!"

Chester regarded me coolly. "You're really very excitable, Harold. That's not good for your blood pressure."

I put my paws around his throat. "Tell me," I said in a low, threatening voice, "or I'll squeeze you till you pop."

"Okay, okay, don't get upset. Now this book tells you everything you've always wanted to know about vampires but were afraid to ask."

Personally, I had never wanted to know anything about vampires, but at the moment, I was afraid to tell that to Chester.

"I still don't understand what vampires have to do with our little furry friend."

"One," Chester said, "vampires do not sleep at night. They sleep only during the day. The same holds true for this rabbit. Two, vampires can get in and out of locked rooms. Bunnicula gets in and out of his locked cage."

This was beginning to interest me. "Didn't you say something about the refrigerator?"

"That's right. He got the refrigerator open . . . all by himself. Three, vampires have long pointed teeth. They're called fangs."

"Well, don't we have fangs?"

"No, we have canines. That's different."

"What's different about it?"

"Fangs are more pointed, and vampires use fangs to bite people on the neck."

"Yech! Who'd want to do that?"

"Vampires would, that's who."

"Wait a minute. I saw Mrs. Monroe bite Mr.

Monroe on the neck once. Does that mean she's a vampire?"

"Boy, are you dumb. She's not a vampire. She's a lawyer."

"She bites necks."

"I don't think that's quite the same thing. Now, Bunnicula does not bite people on the neck. At least, not so far. But he does bite vegetables . . ."

"On the neck?" I asked.

"Vegetables don't have necks, Harold. Vegetables are like that. It's like dogs. Dogs don't have brains. Dogs are like that."

"Oh yeah?" I said. "Of course he bites vegetables. All rabbits bite vegetables."

"He *bites* them, Harold, but he does not eat them. That tomato was all white. What does that mean?"

"It means . . . that he paints vegetables?" I ventured.

"It means he bites vegetables to make a hole in them, and then he sucks out all the juices."

"But what about all the lettuce and carrots that Toby has been feeding him in his cage?"

"Ah ha, what indeed!" Chester said. "Look at

this!" Whereupon, he stuck his paw under the chair cushion and brought out with a flourish an assortment of strange white objects. Some of them looked like unironed handkerchiefs, and the others . . . well, the others didn't look like anything I'd ever seen before.

"What are they?" I asked.

Chester smiled. "Lettuce and carrots," he said. "*White* lettuce and carrots. I found them hidden behind his cage."

I was aghast. What did it all mean? Could Chester be right? Was this harmless looking little ball of fluff really a vampire? Just then, Chester let out a yelp.

"Look," he said, "the cage is empty again. Oh, we're fools, we're fools! We've let him get out of our sight. It's your fault."

"My fault! You're the one who took twenty minutes to sit down."

"Well, if you hadn't knocked me off in the first place—"

"Wait a minute, why are we arguing? Let's find Bunnicula."

Just then, we heard a click in the kitchen.

"Refrigerator," I whispered. Chester nodded. We jumped down and moved cautiously to the kitchen door.

"Sshhh," Chester warned unnecessarily as we crept along, "don't make any noise. We don't want him to hear us coming."

"Obviously," I retorted.

The light went out under the door.

"He must have closed the refrigerator," Chester said. "Easy now." We pushed the door open. The kitchen was dark. There was not a sound.

"Pssst, Chester . . ."

"What?"

"I can't see."

"I can. But I can't see *him.*"

"He's not here."

There was a soft scamper across the linoleum, and we turned just in time to see a little white tail bounce out the door into the living room.

"Drat! We've missed him. Come on, Harold, let's see if we can catch up with him." Chester started toward the door.

"Wait, Chester, what's that on the floor by the refrigerator?"

He turned. This new object interested him more than following Bunnicula. "Watch out," he said, "I'll take care of this." He slunk across the room slowly, muscles taut, eyes alert. When he was about six inches away, he stuck out his paw, closed his eyes and batted at the object tentatively. I don't think he made any contact.

"Get closer," I said.

Chester's eyes popped open. "Who's the cat here?" he asked. "I know what I'm doing." And he proceeded to bat the air three more times.

"What is it?" I squealed, as my throat contracted in fear.

"I don't know yet, but whatever it is, it's not alive."

"Oh boy, if I wait for you, we'll be here all night." I walked bravely to the object and sniffed it.

"Well?" asked Chester.

"Beats me."

Chester came closer. After a moment of close examination, he gasped.

I jumped. I could feel my heart pounding in my chest.

"Harold . . ." Chester blurted.

"What? What?"

"It's . . ."

"Yes?"

"It's . . ."

"What is it, Chester?!"

"It's a white zucchini!"

FIVE

Chester Goes into His Act

THE next morning, I was awakened by a scream.

"Robert! Robert, come down here right away. There's something wrong in the kitchen!"

For a moment, panic seized me. I thought she'd run out of dog food. But then I remembered the events of the previous evening.

Mr. Monroe came bounding down the stairs. "Chester! Chester!" I cried. "Did you see Mr. Monroe? His face has turned white! It's Bunnicula, isn't it?"

"No," he said calmly, "it's shaving cream, you idiot."

By now, the excitement in the kitchen was at full throttle. The table was covered with Bunnicula's handiwork. There were white beans and white peas and white squash and white tomatoes and white lettuce and white zucchini.

"What can it mean, Robert?" Mrs. Monroe was saying. "I'm getting worried. One tomato is a curiosity, but this is unheard of."

"There must be something wrong with our refrigerator. That's it. It's turning all the vegetables white."

"But look," she said, "I left these tomatoes on the windowsill, and they're white too. And this squash I left in the bowl on the table."

At that moment, Pete and Toby came into the kitchen.

"Holy cow! What's going on?"

"Hey! Maybe it's a vegetable blight, Mom."

"Could that be, Robert? Did you ever hear of anything like that?"

"Well . . . uh . . . no, actually . . . that is, I've heard of blight, but nothing like this."

Chester leaned my way. "This will take forever if we leave it up to them. Sometimes, human beings can be so slow." I started to answer him, but he was heading for the table.

"What about that friend of yours in the Agriculture Department?"

"Oh, Tom Cragin?"

"Could we call him and ask him if we're doing something wrong?"

"It's DDT, Mom," Peter interjected, "I know about this stuff. It's because you buy vegetables that aren't organic."

"All vegetables are organic, Peter," Mrs. Monroe replied.

"That's not what my teacher says. See, Toby, I told you this would happen. They're using chemicals on our food, and if you're not careful, you'll turn white, too."

"Like Dad?"

"Robert, couldn't you take that shaving cream off your face?"

"Oh yes, of course. Where's my towel? I know I brought it down with me."

For that matter, where was Chester? I'd seen

him going toward the table, but I'd lost track of him listening to all that talk about DDT. I just hoped they didn't use any of that stuff where they grew chocolate cupcakes.

"Pete, did you take my towel?"

"Why would I take your towel, Dad? I don't shave."

Just then, the door swung open. I could not believe my eyes. There was Chester, with Mr. Monroe's towel draped across his back and tied under his neck like a cape. That was strange enough, but on his face was an expression that sent chills down my spine. His eyes were wide and staring. The corners of his mouth were pulled back in an evil grimace. His teeth were bared and gleaming in the morning light. He cackled menacingly and threw back his head as if he were laughing at all of us. I thought he'd completely lost his mind.

"There's my towel. What's the matter, Chester, were you cold?" Mr. Monroe bent down to take the towel from Chester. Before he could lay his hands on it, Chester flipped over onto his back, closed his eyes and folded his paws over his chest.

It was a hideous sight. He opened his eyes wide. With paws outstretched, he . . . slowly . . . lifted . . . his . . . head . . . his eyes glazed and vacant. Soon the upper half of his body followed, all in one smooth flow, until he was in a sitting position.

"Hey, Dad, did you leave your brandy glass out last night? Chester is acting a little weird."

"Well, son, cats are funny creatures . . ."

I glanced at Chester. He wasn't laughing.

"Psst, Chester. What are you up to?"

"I'm a vampire, you dolt. Can't you tell? I'm trying to warn them."

"Well, it's not working. You'd better think of something else." Chester frowned, apparently deep in thought.

". . . so you see, Toby," Mr. Monroe was explaining, "all cats are as individual as all people. Maybe he just wants to get our attention. Isn't that right, kitty-cat?" Ordinarily, Chester would have left the room upon being called "kitty-cat," but he was lost in thought.

"Come on, Chester, give me back my towel." Mr. Monroe moved toward Chester. Chester's

eyes lit up. He looked at me and smiled. I sensed I was not going to like what he had in mind. I was toying with the notion of slinking under the table when Chester fixed me with his eyes. How deep they were, like black pools. I felt myself floating, lost in them, my will no longer my own. I felt an inexplicable urge to murmur "Yes, Master," when he walked slowly, steadily toward me. As he drew nearer, I found myself unable to move. He stopped before me, never taking his gaze from me, and lunged.

"YEOW!!!"

"Mom, Chester bit Harold on the neck!"

"Aw, that wasn't a real bite, was it Chester? That was a love bite. Isn't that cute?"

Love bite, my foot. That hurt!

"Chester, what's the matter with you?" I sputtered. "Do I look like a tomato?"

"Oh, it doesn't matter anyway, Harold. They don't understand. How can human beings read the same books I do and still be so thick?"

Our conversation was interrupted. Mrs. Monroe picked Chester up and cuddled him. I was praying she would not add insult to injury by kissing his nose, which he hates more than anything.

"Poor Chester, do you need a little love? Do you know what I'm going to do, you big ball of fuzz, you?" Oh, oh. I could tell what was coming. "I'm going to kiss you on your little nose." Yep, I could tell that was coming, all right. Chester knew better than to resist. He went limp in Mrs. Monroe's arms. Mr. Monroe took his towel off Chester.

"I still don't know why he's wearing my towel," he said.

"I think he must be cold, dear. Here's your towel. Why don't you get his kitty sweater . . ." Chester looked ill. ". . . and he can wear that all day."

As Chester was being buttoned into his bright yellow sweater (with little purple mice in cowboy hats all over it), Mr. Monroe said, "What about those vegetables? Shall I speak to Tom Cragin?"

"Yes, dear," Mrs. Monroe said, "why don't you? I'm sure there's some explanation. In the meantime, I'll change markets. To tell you the truth, I'm really much more worried about Chester. We'd better keep our eye on him."

CHESTER and I did not speak until late afternoon. I was busy nursing my neck, and Chester was busy hiding under the sofa, too embarrassed to be seen. When we did speak at last, it was a brief exchange.

"Hey, Chester," I called when he finally crawled out from under, "we don't have to worry about any vampire bunnies anymore. All you have to do is stand outside his cage in that sweater, and he'll laugh himself to death."

Chester was not amused. "That's right, make fun. All of you. No one understands. I tried to warn them, and they wouldn't heed. Now, I'm going to take matters into my own hands."

Whereupon, Chester and his sixteen purple mice went into the kitchen for dinner.

[SIX]

Harold Helps Out

THAT night, I had an uneasy sleep. Strange noises emanated from downstairs. It sounded like toenails clicking back and forth on the floor. It must be Bunnicula making his midnight run, I thought, although I'd never known him to make a sound. And I smelled the funniest odor in the air—something familiar, though I couldn't place it. As the night progressed, it grew stronger and stronger until finally it tickled my nose and I sneezed myself awake. I jumped off Toby's bed, still sniffling, and headed down the stairs for the living room to find Chester, to see if he could smell it, too.

The odor grew even stronger as I approached

the living room. Standing in the doorway was Chester, a strange pendant hanging from his neck.

"Phew, Chester," I said, "what are you wearing that awful thing for? It smells!"

"Of course it smells," he replied. "Here, I made one for you, too. Put it on."

"Are you kidding? That thing smells like garlic."

"It is garlic," Chester stated matter-of-factly.

"Why are you wearing garlic?" I asked, thinking that by this time Chester was capable of anything. As we walked into the living room, I tripped on another piece of garlic lying in the doorway.

"Careful," said Chester, "watch your step."

I surveyed the room and saw that it was strewn with garlic. On the doorways . . . over the windows . . . and around Bunnicula's cage. The poor little fellow had buried his nose as far as possible under his blanket.

I was about to follow his example and return to Toby's bed to bury my nose under the blankets when Chester grabbed my tail with his teeth.

"You're not leaving this room until you put

this on," he grumbled at me. I think that's what he said. I wasn't sure because he had my tail in his mouth.

"It's not polite to talk with your mouth full,

Chester. Drop that tail." Meanwhile, my eyes were beginning to water.

"Listen," Chester snapped at me (fortunately letting go of my tail first), "the book said to use garlic."

"What book?" I asked. *"The Joy of Cooking?"*

Chester continued, *"The Mark of the Vampire* says garlic renders vampires immobile."

"What does that mean?"

"It means they can't go anywhere if there's garlic around."

"Well, I've got news for you, Chester. I can't go anywhere either. The smell is killing me—"

"But you've got to put it on; it says so in the book. If you don't put it on, I'll put it on for you."

"Doe, Chester," I said as my nose suddenly and involuntarily closed, "I'be leaving dis roob right dow." And I did.

I was so sick to my stomach from the aroma that I decided to spend the early morning hours outdoors. As dawn approached, it seemed that it would be a peaceful day. The sky was clear, the birds were singing, and I felt contented after my difficult night just to be lying in the grass, feeling the ladybugs crawl up my ears. Suddenly, the calm was broken. Strange piercing screams came from the area of the kitchen. Not again, I thought. What's turned white now?

As it happened, it was Chester. There in the sink, lathered with soap, was the feline detective, yelling his head off. Mrs. Monroe was scrubbing him vigorously and, from the sound of her voice, was in the middle of a long lecture.

"I don't know what's gotten into you, Chester. You never played with garlic before. I thought you hated the smell of it, and here you've gotten it all over yourself. Stop wriggling, you'll get soap in your eyes. If you want to chew on something, I'll get you some catnip. But stay out of my herbs!" Then she rinsed him off, rubbed him with a towel, and plunked him down in front of the stove to finish drying.

"Shut the door," he hissed at me. "I'm freezing. That silly woman, doesn't she know *cats don't get baths?*"

"What do you mean? I get baths all the time," I said, closing the door with my back foot.

"That's because you're too dumb to bathe yourself. Cats always bathe themselves, it's a rule. Everyone knows that."

"Well, at least it smells nice in here again." I sniffed as I settled down next to Chester by the stove. "And it's all toasty warm here in the kitchen."

"Sure it smells nice again," he said, "but now the house isn't safe anymore."

"What do you mean?" I asked, getting closer.

"I mean, it worked last night. The garlic worked. No more vegetables turned white, did they?"

"No, but . . ."

"That means Bunnicula didn't get out of his cage last night."

"Maybe he was just tired," I said, "or maybe he was full."

"Don't be ridiculous," he replied. "It was the garlic. He *couldn't* leave his cage. But tonight he'll be free to roam again, and I've got to find a way to stop him that isn't smelly."

Mr. and Mrs. Monroe were hurrying in and out of the room, stepping over us, late for work. Mrs. Monroe yelled up to Toby, "Don't forget to take the steak out of the freezer when you get home today, Toby, and leave it on the table to defrost. And this time, remember to put a plate under it."

Chester's ears perked up. "Of course!" he said, "that's what I'll do." And he strolled past me with a knowing smile. Mrs. Monroe turned off the stove and left the room. It was too much for me to figure out, so I went to sleep on the nice, warm kitchen floor.

I was awakened by a bite on the ear. Chester was sitting by me, looking very impatient.

"Boy, nothing wakes you up," he said. "I've been yelling and poking at you for ten minutes."

"I was dreaming," I answered defensively, "about a place where there weren't any cats around to bother nice dogs and wake them up when they needed their rest."

"You can finish sleeping later," he said crisply. "Right now, you have to help me."

"Do what?" I asked.

"Get Bunnicula out of the cage."

I sprang back. "Get him out of the cage?! I thought that was what you didn't want. I thought you said he was dangerous. What if he attacks me?"

"Aren't you ashamed?" Chester replied. "Afraid of a harmless little bunny?"

"Harmless? I thought you said he was a threat to this house and everyone in it. Isn't that what you said? Isn't that what we've been talking about all this time?"

"He is a threat, but only at night. During the day he's just a very sleepy rabbit, and that's why we have to do it now, while the sun is still up. Follow me," he said. "There isn't much time. Toby stayed down here forever, and the others will be home soon. Boy, you must have been tired, Harold. You slept through lunch."

I followed Chester into the living room. My heart was pounding as he unlocked the cage door with his paw. (It looked as if he'd had years of experience opening locks.)

The door swung open; Bunnicula was sleeping peacefully. He did, however, look a little green around the gills, probably from the garlic. I was just wondering how a rabbit could have gills when Chester said, "Okay, Harold, do your stuff while I get what I need from the kitchen."

"Well, what do you want me to do? I can't read your mind."

"Get him out of the cage and onto the floor, and I'll be right back," Chester said.

What? What?

"What?" I verbalized. "How am I supposed to do that?"

"Use your head," he answered. And he was gone. Looking at the cage, I realized that was precisely what I would have to do.

Until this moment, I had never had to face the possibility of actual physical contact with a real, live rabbit. I looked upon my chore reluctantly. I seemed to recall my grandfather telling me that one picked a rabbit up by its neck with one's teeth. This I attempted, though the very idea set my stomach churning. I squeezed my head through the tiny door and gently placed my teeth around the skin of the bunny's neck. To avoid any suggestion of violence (I've never been one for the sport of hunting), I preferred to think of myself as the creature's mother, carrying it off to safety.

Unfortunately, I couldn't carry it anywhere, for once my head was in the cage, it wouldn't come out again. I could go neither forward nor backward.

At that moment, Chester appeared at the door, carrying in his mouth what looked every bit like a nice, big, juicy raw steak. My eyes popped, my teeth dropped Bunnicula, my mouth opened, and I began to drool. After all, I *had* missed lunch.

"Chester, what are you doing with that steak?"

"Haven't you gotten him out of there yet?"

"I can't get either of us out of here. My head's stuck."

"Oh, Harold, sometimes I despair. Here, I'll get you both out. I should have done everything myself."

He came over, dropped the steak just a few feet away from me, and climbed up on my shoulders. "You pull your head out while I push against the cage."

"Who gets the steak?" I asked.

"Don't worry about the steak, Harold. Just pull."

"I would have more motivation if I knew who

is to get the steak."

Chester ignored me. I pulled. He pushed. I felt something go POP! We all fell in a jumble: Chester, the cage, Bunnicula, and me. When I looked around, Bunnicula was lying next to me, still sound asleep.

"There you are," I said. "We got him out. Now, let's eat."

"No dice," Chester said. "Just read this to me so I'll be sure I'm doing it right." And he handed me a book. *That* book, *again.*

"Start at the top of the page," Chester said, as he picked up the steak.

"Why don't *you* read, and I'll hold the steak?"

"Mmphph," Chester replied. I took it to mean that I was to start reading.

" 'To destroy the vampire and end his reign of terror, it is necessary to pound a sharp stake . . .' "

Chester interrupted. "A sharp steak?" he asked. "What does that mean?"

"I'll taste it and tell you if it's sharp," I offered.

"Oh, never mind. This will do. It's sirloin. Keep reading."

" '. . . to pound a sharp stake into the vampire's heart. This must be done during the daylight hours, when the vampire has no powers.' "

"Okay," he said, "this is it. I'm sorry I had to go this far, but if they'd listened, this wouldn't have been necessary." He dragged the steak across the floor and laid it across the inert bunny. Then with his paws, he began to hit the steak.

"Are you sure this is what they mean, Chester?"

"Am I anywhere near his heart?" he asked.

"It's hard to tell," I said. "All I can really see are his nose and his ears. You know, he's really sort of cute."

Chester was getting that glint in his eyes again. He was pounding away at the steak, harder and harder.

"Be careful," I cried, "you'll hurt him."

Chester increased his attack. I was really getting worried when the door opened and Mr. and Mrs. Monroe were suddenly with us in the room.

"Chester!" Mrs. Monroe screamed. "What are you doing with my dinner? Robert, get that steak away from Chester. And what's the matter with Bunnicula? Why is he on the floor?"

Mr. Monroe took the beautiful steak away. I

wished it a fond farewell with tears in my eyes. As the kitchen door swung open, Chester whispered with cold determination, "All right, the last resort!" and dashed into the kitchen. Seconds later, he was back, carrying his water dish between his teeth. He ran toward Bunnicula and with a mad yowl threw the dish of water at the rabbit. Unfortunately, he was so hysterical that his aim was not the best. With water dripping from my ears, I watched Mrs. Monroe pick Chester up by the scruff of his neck and toss him unceremoniously out the front door.

"Robert, we are going to have to do something about that cat. Look at this mess. Dinner's ruined, the poor bunny is out of his cage, and Harold is sopping wet." I tried to look as pathetic as I knew how.

"Aw, poor Harold," Mrs. Monroe cooed as she dried me off. "You've had a rough day . . . you and Bunnicula. I don't know what's the matter with your friend. But unless he learns how to behave, he'll just have to spend the night outside."

Mr. Monroe meanwhile had restored Bunnicula

to his cage and the cage to the windowsill. I couldn't believe it when I saw that Bunnicula was still asleep.

"Ann," Mr. Monroe said, "the steak is ruined. Why don't we let Harold have it? He deserves a treat anyway, don't you, ol' boy?"

I panted appropriately.

AFTER my delicious dinner, I turned my attention to the book still lying open on the floor.

" 'Another method of destroying the vampire is to immerse the body in water. The body will then shrivel and disappear, as the vampire emits one last scream of terror.' "

Whew, I thought, so that's what he was trying to do. Thank goodness he missed. I had no regrets about missing a scene like that. Poor Bunnicula.

I looked over toward the cage, and there on the other side of the window was a pathetic tabby face looking in. His little nose was pressed against the window. I couldn't hear him, but from the movement of his lips, I could see he was very unhappy. Poor Chester.

As for me, Mrs. Monroe spent the evening

petting me and the family chatted with me all night long. And of course, I'd had my yummy steak dinner. So . . . it wasn't such a bad day after all.

Except that now my steak was all gone. Poor Harold.

SEVEN

A (New) Friend in Need

IN the days that followed, Chester's behavior was exemplary. He purred and he cooed and he cleaned his paws. And he rubbed up against everyone's legs to show what a good boy he was. I was getting worried. Chester acts that way only when he has something devious in the back of his mind. But I didn't know what it was. He had tried everything in the book to get rid of vampires, and all his efforts had failed. But I knew from the expression on his face that something was definitely up. Of course, I didn't know for certain because he had not spoken to me since the steak incident. I guess he realized that my heart just wasn't in the destruction of the bunny vampire.

In fact, I was beginning to like the little fellow.

The Monroes were relieved by Chester's improved behavior. They didn't know how to account for his strange doings but, to their credit, they were willing to let bygones be bygones. The only disturbing factor in all our lives was the reappearance of the white vegetables each morning in the kitchen. And yet, after a few days, even that stopped and life seemed to return to normal.

One evening, I dropped by Bunnicula's cage to chat. I'd found myself doing that more and more since Chester had stopped talking to me. Of course, Bunnicula didn't talk back, but he *was* a good listener. I'd begun to think of him as a friend—a strange one, granted—but one can't always choose one's friends. I was distressed this particular evening to see that he was dragging his ears, as it were. He looked tired and listless. I felt his nose and it seemed a little warmer than it should have been. I became alarmed.

I ran over to Toby who was doing a picture puzzle on the floor and began to bark—something

I do only in cases of extreme emergency, since even I do not care for the sound.

"What's the matter, Harold?" Toby asked without moving. "Are there burglers?"

I ran to the cage and looked at Bunnicula. I looked back at Toby and whimpered. Toby just looked confused.

"Do you want to play with Bunnicula? Shall I take him out of the cage?"

"Woof," I responded, indicating, I hoped, that that was indeed what he should do.

"I'll ask Mom and Dad, Harold. You wait here." He was back in a minute, shaking his head. "I'm sorry, Harold, but Mom says you can't play with the rabbit. It causes too much commotion."

I looked down at the floor and whimpered again.

"Sorry, Harold, maybe later when we're all in here together."

I regarded Bunnicula whose eyes met mine. He gave a little shudder, and I felt like crying. My friend was sick, and I didn't know what to do. I wished I could tell Chester, but I knew it was no use. He was just too mad at me. I would have

to sort this one out on my own.

That night, I couldn't sleep worrying about Bunnicula. I decided to go downstairs and check on his condition. What I saw when I entered the living room horrified me. Bunnicula was out of his cage on the floor, while Chester stood in front of him, a piece of garlic around his neck and his arms outstretched, blocking the kitchen door. Suddenly, it all fell into place. Chester was starving Bunnicula! Of course, *that's* why he seemed so listless, and that's why the vegetables had stopped turning white. Chester had made it impossible for Bunnicula to eat.

"Chester!" I cried.

Chester jumped a very high jump.

"What are you doing down here?" he spat at me, as he landed.

"I know what you're doing, Chester, and the jig is up. That little bunny never hurt anybody. All he's doing is eating his own way. What do you care if he drains a few vegetables?"

"He's a vampire!" Chester snarled. "Today, vegetables. Tomorrow . . . the world!"

"I think perhaps you're overstating your case," I suggested cautiously.

"Go back to bed, Harold. This is larger than the two of us. It may seem harsh, but I'm only being cruel to be kind."

Who's he being kind to? I wondered, as I went back upstairs. The tomatoes and zucchinis of the world? Maybe a few cabbages? It just didn't make sense. But I could see I wasn't going to get anywhere with Chester tonight. Tomorrow, however, would be another story, and I was determined that, by hook or by crook, my friend Bunnicula would eat by sundown the next day.

EIGHT

Disaster in the Dining Room

I REALIZED that there was nothing I could do for Bunnicula during the day, since he was sleeping. But that gave me time to plan my strategy. At first, I thought I would bring food to his cage, but then it occurred to me that Chester must be taking everything away that was given to him. Pete and Toby usually left lettuce for Bunnicula during the day while he was sleeping, and Chester, ever watchful, probably nabbed it each evening just before the rabbit woke. No, there would have to be another way.

I thought and thought all afternoon, and I

could see that Chester had done a good job of isolating Bunnicula from his food. There was no way I could think of to overcome Chester's game plan. As evening drew closer and I grew more and more frantic, I stumbled into the dining room . . . and saw the answer to my problems sitting before me on the table. It was a big bowl of salad! All I had to do was get Bunnicula to the salad and let him get his fill before the family came in to eat. With that funny white dressing on it, they would never notice if a few vegetables were white.

I ran to the hallway to check the clock. Six fifteen. It would be fifteen minutes before the sun went down and Bunnicula woke up. I would then need at least five minutes to get him from his cage to the table and feed him. All I had to do was make sure no one came into the room until he had finished. I needed a good twenty minutes, at least.

I went back into the living room. Chester was asleep on his brown velvet chair, shedding in his sleep, still worn out from the previous night's activities. I checked upstairs. Toby was reading in his room, the last chapter of *Treasure Island,* I noted. Pete, who should have been doing his homework, was listening to records in his room.

I ran down to the kitchen.

"Hello, Harold," Mrs. Monroe said as I came through the door. "What's new?"

Other than a rabbit starving in the next room and an imminent attack on your salad bowl, nothing, I thought. I stood at her feet and panted. She scratched my head. This gave me a moment to check out how far she was in her cooking.

"Sorry, Harold," she said. "I have to baste this chicken." I noticed the oven timer still had thirty-five minutes to go. It'll be tight, I thought, but I can make it. Now, where is Mr. Monroe?

I went to the front door and whimpered loudly. Mrs. Monroe followed me.

"Are you waiting for Daddy, Harold? He'll be home soon."

Soon isn't good enough. *How* soon? I whimpered again.

"Patience, boy. He's late at a school meeting. He should be here any time."

She went back into the kitchen and I checked the clock. Six twenty-five. It was getting dark and

BUNNICULA

Chester was still asleep. Time to swing into action.

Having watched Chester undo the lock on Bunnicula's cage and having participated in that unfortunate steak episode some days earlier, I knew I would have no problem getting Bunnicula out. I just had to be a little more careful where I positioned my head so that I wouldn't find myself in the humiliating predicament of getting stuck a second time. My timing was perfect. With Bunnicula swinging peacefully from my teeth, I made my way stealthily toward the dining room as the last rays of sunlight gave way to the dark of night. Once inside the dining room door, Bunnicula awakened in great bewilderment. It is not everyday, after all, that one finds oneself, upon awakening, hanging from the jaws of a fellow creature—even so caring and gentle a creature as myself.

Bunnicula opened his eyes wide and turned his face, as best he could, to me. I jumped up onto the nearest chair and placed the rabbit safely on the table's edge.

"Okay," I whispered, "there's your dinner. Go to it! Get your fill as fast as you can, poor bunny.

I'll stand guard." I don't know that Bunnicula fully understood what was going on, but the sight of the vegetables piled high in the center of the table sent him scurrying in their direction. He was *very* hungry!

As luck would have it (and as I should have anticipated), Chester's sense of timing was as astute as my own. No sooner had Bunnicula reached the edge of the salad bowl than the door swung open and Chester bounded into the room. He surveyed the scene frantically. I was unable to act fast enough. Upon seeing Bunnicula about to enjoy his first bit of nourishment in days, Chester leaped across the table, seemingly without touching floor, chairs, or anything else between himself and our furry friend and landed directly on top of the bunny.

"Oh no, you don't!" he shrieked. Bunnicula, not sure what to do, jumped high in the air and landed, with a great scattering of greens, smack in the center of the salad bowl. Lettuce and tomatoes and carrots and cucumbers went flying all over the table and onto the floor. Chester flattened his ears, wiggled his rear end and smiled

in anticipation. To cat observers, this is known as the "attack position."

"Run, Bunnicula!" I shouted. Bunnicula turned in my direction, as if to ask where.

"Anywhere!" I cried. "Just get out of his way!"

Chester sprang.

Bunnicula jumped.

And in the flash of a second, they had changed positions. Chester now found himself flat on his back (owing to the slipperiness of the salad dressing) in the bowl. And Bunnicula, too dazed to even think about food now, hovered quivering on the table.

Chester was having a great deal of difficulty getting back on his feet, but I knew it was only a matter of seconds before he'd attack again. And I knew also that Bunnicula was too petrified to do anything to save himself. So I did the only thing I could: I barked. Very loudly and very rapidly.

The whole family rushed through the doors. Mr. Monroe must have just come home because his coat was still on.

"Oh, no!" cried Mrs. Monroe. "That's it, Chester. This is Chester's last stand!"

Chester rolled his eyes heavenward and didn't even try to move.

"Mom," said Toby, tugging at his mother's arm, "look at Bunnicula. How did he get out of his cage? He looks scared."

"Of course, he's scared," Mrs. Monroe said. "We probably forgot to latch his cage and he got out. And I think Chester has been chasing him."

Toby put his face close to the rabbit. "Mom, doesn't Bunnicula look kinda sick?"

"We'd better take them all to the vet to see if any damage was done," she answered.

I started to whimper. No need for *me* to go to the vet.

Mr. Monroe patted my head. "We may as well take Harold along," he said. "He's probably due for his shots."

Mrs. Monroe carefully picked Chester out of the salad bowl and carried him by the scruff of the neck to the kitchen. "I'm going to give Chester a quick bath," she said to Mr. Monroe. "Why don't you put together a fresh salad? Toby, you and Peter put Bunnicula back in his cage and

[90]

then clean up the table."

I didn't stick around for an assignment. This was not the time to be in the way.

And besides, I now had a whole evening and night ruined worrying about the next morning's visit to the vet. This little effort of mine, I thought, has been a disaster in more ways than one.

NINE

All's Well that Ends Well . . . Almost

LOOKING back on that night, I remember thinking that this whole mess could never be resolved happily. What would become of Bunnicula, my new friend, who was suffering from starvation? And what of Chester, my old friend, who seemed to have flipped his lid and, if you'll pardon the expression, was in the dog-house with the Monroes? Of far greater concern at that time, of course, was my own future, for on that night all that consumed my thoughts was the fear of the next day's injections! It all seemed hopeless indeed.

But looking back on the next *day,* I can tell you that happy endings are possible, even in situations as fraught with complications as this one was.

Early the next morning, we all piled into the car, some of us with greater reluctance than others, and trundled off to the vet. And by afternoon, we were on our way to solving our problems.

The vet worked everything out very nicely. He discovered that Bunnicula was suffering from extreme hunger. (*I* could have told him that.) Rather than jar his fragile stomach with solid foods, the doctor decided he should be put on a liquid diet until he got better. So Bunnicula was immediately given some carrot juice, which he drank eagerly. After he finished, he looked over at me with a great grin on his face and winked.

Chester was diagnosed as being emotionally overwrought. It was suggested that he start sessions with a cat psychiatrist to work out what the doctor called a case of sibling rivalry with Bunnicula. I asked Chester later what a sibling was, but he wasn't speaking to me. So I looked it up. It's like a brother or sister. And sibling rivalry means you are competing with your brother or sister for attention. I wasn't sure this was Chester's problem, but it sure explained a lot about Toby and Pete.

As for me . . . well, I came out the best. Dr. Wasserman was all set to give me my shots when the nurse came in with my card.

"Wait, doctor, this dog doesn't need his shots yet. It's too soon."

So I got a pat on the head and a doggie-pop instead.

THESE days, everything is back to normal in the Monroe household—almost. Bunnicula liked his liquid diet so much that the Monroes have kept him on it. And oddly enough, there have been no problems with vegetables mysteriously turning white since. Chester, of course, insists that this proves his theory.

"Obviously, Harold, the liquified vegetables take the place of the vegetable juices, so Bunnicula has no need to go roaming anymore."

"Then he's not a vampire," I said.

"Nonsense. He's a vampire all right. But he's a modern vampire. He gets his juices from a blender."

"Case closed, Sherlock?" I queried.

"Case closed."

"Oh, Chester . . ."

"Yes, Harold?"

"What are those two funny marks on your neck?"

Chester jumped and I laughed. "Very funny," he said as he began to bathe his tail, "very funny."

The Monroes never knew anything of Chester's theory. They changed markets and to this day believe they were the victims of a curious vegetable blight.

Bunnicula and I have become good friends. He still doesn't say anything, but he snuggles up next to me by the fireplace and we take long cozy snoozes together. One night, I sang him a lullaby in the obscure dialect of his homeland, and he slept very peacefully. It was that night that cemented our friendship.

Now—about Chester. I said that everything

was back to normal—almost. Naturally, Chester is the "almost." He has been seeing his psychiatrist, Dr. Verrückt Katz, twice a week for some time now. He takes his therapy *very* seriously.

The other morning, I was trying to get a little sleep, when Chester came over and nudged me in the ribs.

"Harold, do you realize we've never really communicated? I mean *really* communicated?"

I opened one eye cautiously.

"And in order to communicate, Harold, you have to really be in touch with yourself. Are you in touch with yourself, Harold? Can you look yourself in the mirror and say, 'I know who I am. I am in touch with the me-ness that is me, and I can reach out to the you-ness that is you'?"

I closed my eye. I'm used to it by now. He talks like that all the time. He no longer reads Edgar Allan Poe at night. And once he concluded that he had been right about Bunnicula, there has been no more talk about vampires. *The Mark of the Vampire* sits, its usefulness obsolete, on its shelf. Right now, he's reading *Finding Yourself*

by Screaming a Lot, and the other night, when I heard the most awful noise coming from the basement, I didn't even bat an eyelid. I knew it was just Chester "finding himself," as he calls it. He explains to me that he's getting in touch with his kittenhood. And I've told him that's fine—just to let me know when he's going to do it, so I can be elsewhere. I've had enough trouble from Chester's adventures.

SO that's my story. And the story of a mysterious stranger who no longer seems quite so mysterious and who is definitely no longer a stranger. I've presented the facts as clearly as I could, and I leave it to you, dear reader, to draw your own conclusions.

I must now bring this narrative to a close, since it is Friday night—Toby's night to stay up late and read—and I can hear the crinkling of cellophane. I can only hope it covers two chocolate cupcakes with cream filling.

Writing
BUNNICULA
The Story Behind the Story

by JAMES HOWE

for Mark

What happened I do not remember now. Not all of it, or even most. Who said what to whom, and why. The details of the days. But the days themselves, these I remember as one long day passing inevitably into one long night.

I am speaking of the days that stretched from July 1977 to June 1978, but the story begins before then—in the spring of 1977, although I can't recall the day or week or month; earlier still, in the fall of 1969, the fall of 1964, in August of 1946. I was born that month, on the second day, in Oneida, New York, the youngest of four brothers and the only one to be born in a hospital and not at home. Debbie, the first child of two, was born ten days later, on the twelfth of August, in a hospital in Boston, Massachusetts. We met at Boston University in the fall of 1964, married in New York City in the fall of 1969, and began to write a children's book in the spring of 1977.

It was evening, just after dinner, when we sat down at our kitchen table, the wooden table I had painted a lustrous tomato-red soon after we'd married, and began to write.

I still have the scrap of paper from that evening. The misspelling and handwriting are hers. Oh, yes, most definitely her scrawl, so like tangled hair it was sometimes impossible to decipher. Were we drinking coffee? There's a stain on the paper that leads me to believe we were. Why do I see her standing at the kitchen sink, her head cocked to the side, her thick black hair falling over one shoulder? Why do I hear her laughing? Is it because she laughed so easily, or is it because in writing the book we were just then beginning, we would laugh so often? I see—or imagine I see—the look in her eyes that said: Who are *we* to think we can write a book? Who were we indeed?

Debbie and I were thirty when we began writing

Brother, Sister, parents, cat,

Bunny found in back row of movie theatre with note in unknown foreign language saying "take take care of my baby."

Count Bunnicula

1. Transylvanian Bunny turns to Vampire at nite
2. Drains Vegetables
3. War with household cat Chester
   reads books on Vampires
   + tries to destroy count Bunnicula
   1. tries to drive a stake thru his heart (Kneading like mouse)
   2. Throw water + bowl at him
   3. wears garlic around his neck + has to be washed. when he gets cut Count B (has eaten his dinner)
   4. mother always catches cat quiet when he's doing it.
   5. pantomimes vampire act — apron + runs from room to room they think he's crazy + take him to the vet.

Chester is setting up his biggest trap that B turns around. so C. has to go to a cat psychiatrist

letter from Chester

Bunnicula. We had met twelve years earlier as freshman theater students. At eighteen, she was an elegant, cosmopolitan New Yorker whose pale complexion, cool beauty, and sense of style made her look as if she'd just stepped off the cover of a fashion magazine. I, on the other hand, looked as if I had just stepped off the bus. With my straight brown hair forever falling over my eyes, and cheeks that turned crimson at the least provocation, I was such an innocent I was dubbed "the hick" by my more sophisticated classmates. We were an unlikely pair. In fact, we weren't a pair at all until the summer between our junior and senior years. I tried dating Debbie our freshman year, but she informed me in no uncertain terms that I was not a likely candidate for her particular life scenario.

"I am destined to marry a doctor and live in Scarsdale," she informed me over dinner at a restaurant I couldn't afford, one that served the kind of heavily sauced, impossible-to-pronounce dishes I imagined would impress someone as glamorous and worldly as she, and which left me stammering and sweaty. "I am not meant to live with an artist in a garret," she went on, delivering the final blow to any thought I might have had of a future with her.

I told her she was crazy to think she could know her future with such certainty. She told me I was crazy to think people had the freedom to deny their destinies. We agreed to think the other crazy and became good friends.

Had we met as children we would have been

able to skip the expensive-dinner part, the wooing and the rejecting, and gone straight to friendship, because my guess is that we would have been friends. Despite appearances, we had a great deal in common.

Although we both loved words and weren't shy about using them, Debbie was—and would always be—far more of a reader than I. From an early age, she read quickly and with understanding. As an adult, it wasn't uncommon for her to read anywhere from ten to twenty books in a week. When it came to reading, I was the tortoise to her hare. If I managed to read one book in a week it was an accomplishment. Besides, when I was a boy, my favorite reading wasn't books but comics and *Mad* magazine. I don't know what kinds of reading Debbie favored as a young girl, but as a teenager and adult she read everything from classics to trash, although she had a special place in her heart for romantic novels, shivery gothics, and historical fiction.

We were both writers as children. Writing was for me a natural extension of the kind of make-believe play I had engaged in with friends or by myself for as long as I can recall. Debbie, too, liked to act out the movies she'd seen or fantasies conjured from books or real life or thin air. She and her

The 1950s. Debbie in Newton, Massachusetts: a studio portrait and a less formal shot taken in the backyard with her brother, Mark. Both photos of me were taken on the back steps of my house in Webster, New York. The beagle was named Patches.

brother, Mark, whiled away many hours spinning stories together. She was always dramatic, always the actress.

I close my eyes and picture her with a feather boa wrapped around her neck, tottering in her mother's high heels and proclaiming from beneath rhinestone-studded sunglasses, "No more interviews!" as her brother, playing the reporter with notebook and pencil in hand, begs the famous movie star to answer just one more question, just one more. "Are the rumors true . . ." he begins, then falters as he waits for her to whisper the rest of his lines to him.

And where am I when this imagined scene is taking place in the backyard of the Smith family's house in Newton, Massachusetts? It might be 1954, 1955. I'm living then in Webster, New York, having moved from Oneida at the age of two. I'm in the fourth grade, playing the part of a monkey in a class play about the jungle; I'm in love with my teacher, Mrs. Kubrich; I'm spending my weekly allowance of twenty-five cents at Bowman's Candy Store on one comic book—*Archie*, probably—and fifteen cents worth of penny candy (buttons, wax lips, jawbreakers, tiny tins of fudge eaten with tiny tin spoons). While Debbie is in the Brownies, I'm in the Cub Scouts, but only for a year. It feels too much like the army, and besides, I'm such a chatterbox I can't stop talking long enough to finish the birdhouse my fellow scouts complete with ease.

It was in the fifth grade, I think, that I was so taken with the idea of vampires that I co-founded—with my friends Terry Frost and Judy Koch—a club called the Vampire Legion. Membership: 3. I don't remember much about the Vampire Legion other than meeting one time in somebody's basement (Judy's, I think), where we turned off the lights, lit candles, and made weird faces at each other. We also published a newspaper called the *Gory Gazette*. I was the editor. Circulation: 3.

I don't know where the fascination with vampires came from, since I don't recall liking horror movies much unless they were played for laughs. The one "scary" movie I remember seeing as a child was *The Egyptian*, which contained a battle scene so bloody it gave me nightmares for weeks. Debbie loved scary movies, even as a child, although her favorite, the fantastical *The Thief of Bagdad*, had only intermittent scary parts. I preferred movies that made me laugh—Abbott and Costello; Dean Martin and Jerry Lewis; Francis the Talking Mule. I admit it: I was a major Three Stooges fan. I just liked to laugh. Growing up in a house of jokers, I got to laugh a lot.

I'm picturing another kitchen table now—the round oak table in the house in Webster where I grew up. This table had what I thought was a shelf located conveniently underneath, the perfect place for depositing food I was too full or disgusted by to eat. Leaning into the table, an innocent look on my face as I chewed air, I would fumble to place half a sandwich there or—the greater challenge—a forkful of despised string beans with mushroom gravy. It never occurred to me that this shelf might serve any purpose other than a home for unwanted food. Never, that is, until I returned from school one afternoon and saw the pile of moldy crusts and hardened green and brown lumps sitting in the middle of the table like Oscar the Grouch's idea of a centerpiece. My mother was at the sink, scrubbing vegetables, her back to me. My heart sank as I tried desperately to comprehend how my secret hiding place could possibly have been discovered. It turned out my "shelf" was really a leaf used to extend the size of the table.

"Didn't you think we might have company one day?" my mother asked. She turned to look at my face, and then burst out laughing.

She loved to laugh, my mother—and that is how I see her now, sitting at that table, with her husband across from her and three of her four sons—myself and my brothers Dave and Doug—completing the circle. My oldest brother, Lee, had gone off to college by the time I was four. I hear my father say, "I heard a good one today." And the joke-telling begins. My brothers pitch in with jokes they've heard. They astound me. They *all* have new jokes to tell. Where do they get them? Why is it I never have any new jokes? It could be because I couldn't then—and still can't—remember jokes to save my life, but it also could be that I just didn't hear them. How was it that they did? How did they manage to come to dinner every night with new material?

I had to do something about it—and I did. I trooped off to the school library and checked out books of jokes and riddles. And every night at six I arrived at the kitchen table armed and ready. Most of my offerings were interrupted by one of my brothers shouting out the punchline or, worse, greeted with stony-faced silence. They were a punishing audience, putting me through an apprenticeship, forcing me to earn my laughs. But when I did manage to get a good one across—ah, the satisfaction! What I discovered was that I didn't really need the joke books. I was a fast thinker—I had to be, growing up in that house—and I often managed to come up with something all my own that made everyone laugh.

I was told I had a "way with words," and my mother always said, "You should be a writer when you grow up."

But I didn't want to be a writer, even though I loved to write. From the time I was ten, I wanted to be an actor. I lulled myself to sleep every night plotting out in great detail the movies I would star in, scripting the interviews and acceptance speeches I would give . . . writing, writing, rewriting. But I didn't think of it as writing. No, it was all in the service of something greater than words: my own glory! Could there have been words grand enough to describe my brilliance! It's a wonder I ever fell asleep at all, considering the energy I poured into constructing the career of the great, the famous . . . Sir Reginald Windsor!

Sir Reginald Windsor was not a character in a story I wrote. He was the actor I imagined myself one day becoming. Before the 1960s, movie stars often changed their names. Marion Michael Morrisson became John Wayne. Roy Fitzgerald turned into Rock Hudson; Bernie Schwartz into

Tony Curtis. But I didn't see myself as a Rock or a Tony. No, I wanted to be the American equivalent of my hero—Sir Laurence Olivier, a British actor of such genius he had been knighted by the Queen. I didn't know you couldn't just call yourself "Sir."

Had Debbie and I known each other then, she might have guided me to a tad less pretentious name, but she would surely have joined in the fantasy, for I have little doubt that she, too, had dreams of being famous. What was it that was so alluring about the spotlight for both of us? Was it a product of having had "famous" fathers? Debbie's father was Lester Smith, a well-known newscaster on WOR Radio from the time the family moved to New York City in 1958, when Debbie was twelve, until he retired years later. My father, while not known to as wide an audience, was an outspoken community leader, first in the Rochester, New York, area and then in Schenectady, New York where my family moved in 1958. My father was a Baptist minister whose activism and liberal views on civil rights, the peace movement, and other social issues of the day made him a highly visible and frequently controversial figure.

If having the particular fathers we did accounted in some part for the attraction to the spot-

light we both felt, it also may have accounted for other things we had in common. Our love of words, for instance. Words were an integral part of our fathers' work. For Debbie's father, the exact use and meaning of words was crucial; the misuse of one word could distort the truth or slant a news report. For my father, words were the very tools with which he constructed a relationship with his congregants and community. Words were used to heighten consciousness, to inspire, to build the bridge between silent thoughts and meaningful actions. My father had studied preaching in its heyday, and he was masterful at it. I may not remember the contents of his sermons (I was too busy counting the squares in the church ceiling or the ladies' hats while he spoke), but I must have been listening, because to this day I can feel his style within my own. There are times I'm writing when it is almost as if his hands were guiding mine.

Because of our fathers, Debbie and I both grew up with an awareness of the world's problems and a sensitivity to its injustices. While religion played a larger part in my life as a child, Debbie's Jewishness played a part in shaping her sensitivity to the plight of the outsider and to the occurrence of injustice. Always protective of her little brother, she was ever on the alert for a perceived unfairness done to him or anyone else she cared about, and if she did see an injustice being done, her defense of the victim would fly from her—passionate, eloquent, dramatic, and heartfelt.

But her sensitivity to injustice and what it was to be an outsider went deeper and was more personal than mere social awareness. For despite her beauty and her sophistication, Debbie wasn't comfortable in the world. She saw herself as different, as an outsider trying to find a way in. I, too, was an outsider. My ease with words, especially in making others laugh, and my hunger for the spotlight masked a shy, sensitive, nonathletic boy who was afraid of being seen as different, of being mocked or excluded. Words were my power, as Debbie's beauty was hers. But words—read, spoken, or written—gave both Debbie and me the tools to try and find our way into a world in which we didn't feel quite at home and the language with which to dream.

Our common dream of becoming actors carried us through high school to the Boston University School of Fine and Applied Arts where, after three years of being friends, we felt our friendship grow into something more. We moved to New York City after graduating in 1968 and married in 1969.

Along the way, we acquired two cats. Debbie named hers, a delicate-looking, long-haired gray tabby, Ganymede, from Shakespeare's *As You Like It*, revealing her romantic, theatrical nature. I named mine, a tiny white kitten we *thought* was a female, Moose, revealing my warped sense of humor. Sadly, Ganymede died from unknown causes only a year after we'd gotten her from the animal shelter. Moose, who lived to be thirteen, revealed his true gender and in a very short time grew from petite to extra-large, fully justifying the name I'd given him.

Both of us loved animals, cats especially. Debbie hadn't grown up with pets, due to her mother's allergies, except for one—a parakeet named Petey. I had grown up with many pets—

dogs, cats, rabbits, hamsters, and a canary named Alice. My favorite book was—and is—*Charlotte's Web* by E. B. White. One of the main reasons for this is that it is about animals and what they might say and do if they acted, spoke, and thought as people do. My favorite movie growing up wasn't a funny one at all, but a sad one about a dog. Had there been videotapes when I was a boy, I'm sure I would have watched *Old Yeller* as many times as I read and reread *Charlotte's Web*.

As an aside, *Charlotte's Web* was published the year I was in the first grade. I remember taking it to my teacher to ask her to read it to the class. She did so, with much delight and a great sense of humor, which she needed since her name was Miss Wilbur! I took it to school with me every year after that through fifth grade, asking each teacher in turn to read it aloud to the class.

While living in our first apartment in Brooklyn Heights—just across the Brooklyn Bridge from Manhattan—Debbie and I acquired another cat to replace Ganymede. This one, a pretty but vacuous and tirelessly irritating part-Siamese Debbie named Gudrun (after a character from D. H. Lawrence's novel *Women in Love*), rounded out our household for several years. Moose never entirely took to Gudrun. He would terrorize her by stationing himself about six feet away from their food dishes and cackling at her every time she tried to eat. When it was his turn to eat (we assumed Gudrun successfully managed to get nourishment only by tiptoeing to the food dishes when Moose was napping in another part of the apartment), Moose would often line up his catnip mice at the side of his dish to keep him company. We never knew if he did this because he was pretending he was throwing a dinner party or because he was imagining the mice were on the menu.

Moose in particular inspired us as we created the character of Chester. Even while writing the last book in the series—*Bunnicula Strikes Again!*—I found myself recalling, over twenty years later, the time I pulled what I thought was a tiny bit of string out of Moose's mouth, only to have it uncoil for about ten feet. Harold's recollection of Chester's looking like a tape dispenser is a mere transposition of the words I remember thinking about Moose at the time.

But, as Harold would say, I digress.

I was talking about the post-college years in New York, when Debbie and I were in our early twenties and baffled by life. During our senior year in college, I faced the fact that, despite my long-time desire to be an actor, I really wasn't all that good at it. While that assessment was fairly accurate, it had no doubt been fostered by a particularly severe professor by the name of Dr. Hobbs, who by the time we graduated had reduced all but the most gifted or determined students to human question marks, curled in on ourselves to face our futures with a diminished sense of self-worth and a hole where our dreams had been.

This professor, who firmly believed he was doing his students a favor by being brutally honest, was fond of saying, "I'm only being cruel to be kind," a line he lifted from Shakespeare's *Hamlet*, and which I in turn lifted from him and gave to Chester in *Bunnicula*.

> *"Go back to bed, Harold. This is larger than the two of us. It may seem harsh, but I'm only being cruel to be kind."*
>
> *Who's he being kind to? I wondered, as I went back upstairs. The tomatoes and zucchinis of the world? Maybe a few cabbages? It just didn't make sense.*

Dr. Hobbs's philosophy of cruelty-for-the-sake-of-kindness didn't make much sense to me, either, especially after four years of college that had prepared me for, as it turned out, nothing. I briefly entertained the notion of becoming a writer. But I couldn't dispel the aura of self-doubt that had been cast over me. In a letter to Debbie dated October 26, 1968, I dismissed the idea of being a writer with these self-deprecating words:

> *I am not an artist, not an actor, not a writer, nothing. Creative I may be, but I'm not going to make my living at it. If I really wanted to be a writer, I'd be reading or writing every spare minute. I've found that the "loner" I always thought I was just doesn't exist. I like people and I like working with them and to shut myself up in a closet and create unpublishable manuscripts is no answer.*

Five year later, Debbie would write about herself in a similar vein in her journal:

> *Jimmy [as I was called by my family growing up and later by Debbie and her family] has convinced himself that I am going to write a novel . . . That's his little fantasy, that I'm going to write something and through that fulfill myself.*

*It's a joke. I've never written anything in my life.
I can't write. I'm terrible at it.*

Yet we both continued to write—mostly frag-
ments, ideas, thoughts, poems, letters, notes to
each other. Nothing serious. Still, I must have decided to take myself seriously at some point, because around this time, I applied to the Columbia
University School of Journalism, thinking that perhaps my mother had been right, after all. Perhaps I
should be a writer when I grew up.

But I was turned down by Columbia, and because I had always been interested in what makes
people tick, I set my sights next on earning a graduate degree in psychology and becoming a thera-
pist. I went back to school during the evenings to
earn undergraduate credits in psychology, took
typing jobs during the day to pay the bills (thank
heavens for that touch-typing class in high
school!), and stayed up late most nights watching
old movies on TV.

There were no VCRs in the early 1970s, no
videotapes, no cable television. But there was *The
Late Show* at 11:30 after the news, and *The Late Late
Show* at one in the morning, and *The Late Late Late
Show* after that. Debbie and I stayed up many a

night to watch our favorites—*The House of Usher* and *The Pit and the Pendulum,* among other adaptations of Edgar Allan Poe stories produced and directed by Roger Corman and frequently starring Vincent Price; and anything, anything at all, produced by the British "house of horror," Hammer Films. These movies, many of them vampire variations starring Christopher Lee, were scary, funny, and often screamingly bad. We loved them beyond reason. We also loved non-horror movies—Sherlock Holmes mysteries starring Basil Rathbone as the famous sleuth; the Marx Brothers' comedies; and the song-and-dance extravaganzas of Fred Astaire and Ginger Rogers. But it was the vampire movies of Christopher Lee—*Dracula: Prince of Darkness; Scars of Dracula; Dracula Has Risen from the Grave,* to name a few—that we were willing to stay up until three in the morning to watch, risking bleary eyes and late arrivals at whatever typing job was currently helping keep the bill collectors from the door.

Debbie worked at an odd assortment of jobs at this time, most of them jobs related to the fashion business. Neither of us was excited about the work we did, so when my applications to graduate school in psychology didn't pan out, we decided to take another stab at making a living in the theater.

Our return to show business took us to an out-door summer stock theater in Danville, Kentucky, called the Pioneer Playhouse. Only in our early twenties, we were cast as the leading man and lead-ing lady of the season and given the opportunity to play everything from young love interests to a middle-aged couple to octogenarians. Along with the others in our company, we also battled spiders the size of small dogs, occasionally onstage during a performance. Many nights, we sat outside our rooms overlooking the theater and watched in awe as aerial ballets were performed by hundreds, perhaps thou-sands, of bats against the backdrop of a deep purple sky. We ate cheese at every meal because, rumor had it, a food delivery truck had broken down in front of the theater and the owners had gotten a deal on huge blocks of cheddar that would otherwise have gone bad in the hot summer sun. We swam at midnight, played poker at all hours, and created a mock 1950s gang, giving ourselves mock 1950s names. I was Flash. Debbie was Dee-Dee.

It was a glorious summer. We returned home by train, an overnight trip during which Moose and Gudrun, who had spent the summer with my brother Dave and his family across the state line

Summer 1971, Pioneer Playhouse. Me, as a young suitor in a play by John Boruff called *The Loud Red Patrick;* Debbie, wearing the kind of beautiful period costume she loved, in Moliere's classic farce, *The Imaginary Invalid;* and the two of us, relaxing during a rehearsal break.

from the theater in Cincinnati, Ohio, howled incessantly from their carriers at the rear of the compartment, to the complaints of all the other passengers who were trying to sleep. We pretended they were someone else's cats and ignored them entirely.

Coming home with new friends and a renewed sense of ourselves as theater people, we threw ourselves into the task of finding work as actors. We

DEBORAH FRANKLIN

Our professional acting photos, called "head shots." Debbie took the stage name of "Franklin" in honor of her grandfather, Frank. My photo caught the eye of a modeling agency and led to my brief career as a model for national magazine ads.

had photographs taken. We read the casting papers— *Show Business* and *Backstage*—and showed up for auditions. We both tried getting work as models; ironically, I was the one to succeed. For a year I worked steadily as a model for ads that appeared in magazines all over the country. To my relatives, at least, I was famous!

In some ways, the most important thing that had been restored to us that summer in Kentucky was a sense of play. With our newest best friends, Annie and Lawrence, who also lived in Brooklyn, we passed many an evening entertaining ourselves by improvising silly song parodies, mock epic poems, absurd plays, and spoofs of TV commercials. When we tired of playing, we speculated endlessly on what our lives might yet become; we still felt a long way from being grown-up. We were children at heart, children at play, the four of us.

And Debbie and I, we were children in adult bodies who, in the spirit of play, would one evening a few years later begin to write a book. We were actors, used to transforming ourselves into other characters, practiced at imagining our ways into other lives, other skins. We were readers. We were writers, but not writers who took themselves seriously. We were watchers of countless horror movies and comedies and musicals spun of tinsel and silk. We were cat-lovers and chocolate-lovers and believers in magic.

A belief in magic is required if you want to be an actor, but it doesn't pay the rent. While I did have my modeling work, the occasional job as a movie extra, and acting stints off-off-Broadway where the salary was subway fare, I still needed those typing jobs to put dinner on the table for Debbie and me, and tuna on the floor for Gudrun and Moose and his lineup of catnip mice.

In 1975, I accepted a job offer from the woman who ran the literary and theatrical agency where I had been working as a temporary typist. The job was fairly mundane; I knew enough about language to recognize that even if you call somebody an assistant, a secretary is a secretary. And I was a secretary. But there was a certain amount of glamour associated with the position and with the business. It wasn't long before I was rubbing shoulders with (or at least taking phone calls from) famous actors and writers, and getting an education in the "real world" of show business and publishing.

At the same time, I wasn't about to let go of my dreams. I just had to pursue them on evenings and weekends. Having become more interested in directing than acting, I went after every opportunity I could find to direct plays at community theaters, on college campuses, and off-off-Broadway, where the salary had gone from seventy cents to a dollar a day to reflect the increase in the cost of two subway tokens.

Debbie frequently acted in the plays I directed, and she tried to find other work as an actress, but her efforts were thwarted—as so much in her life had been thwarted—by the illnesses that had plagued her from the time she was only months old and suffering from terrible earaches and fevers. Her mother remembers the long nights of walking the floor with her, remembers the swelling in her cheek when she was eighteen months old, remembers being told the swelling was nothing to worry about, nothing, just a reaction to fever. But it was more than nothing, and the swelling would appear again, and again, and there would be more long nights to come.

In August of 1976, Debbie and I took the only real vacation we ever had together: two weeks on the New Jersey shore. On her thirtieth birthday, I gave her a pair of diamond stud earrings. The diamonds were small and not of very good quality; they were all I could afford, but Debbie, who had long ago forgotten about being married to a doctor in Scarsdale and seemed quite content to be living, literally, with an artist in a garret, was touched by the gift. And she cried.

"I didn't expect to live to be thirty," she told me.

The swelling in her cheek had years before been diagnosed as a recurrent benign cyst, a condition that had required numerous hospitalizations and surgical interventions, starting when she was fifteen.

While this condition was the worst Debbie suffered, it was not the only one. She was frequently sick with one thing or another; even the common cold hit her harder than it did most people.

When she was ill, books were her best companions. I picture her, stretched out on the sofa in that apartment at the top of the brownstone in Brooklyn Heights where *Bunnicula* was begun, a box of tissues beside her, Gudrun curled up on her lap, a book open in her hands, and there, always within easy reach, a stack of books waiting to be read.

And I think of a play written by a client of the literary agency where I worked. The play is called *Artichoke*, the playwright is Joanna M. Glass. In it, there is a character of a young girl by the name of Lily Agnes. Lily Agnes always wears a particular hat; she refuses to part with it. Whenever she has it on her head, she explains, she is "an island of calm in a turbulent sea." For Debbie, reading was her island of calm in the sea of a life made turbulent by illness and pain.

Looking back at 1976 and 1977, I see my own life as turbulent, albeit in a much more superficial way. Not only was I still working for the literary agency by day, but many of my evenings and weekends were taken up with attending plays and movie screenings that were work-related. Somehow, I found the time to take classes at Hunter College, where I was working toward a master's degree in theater, and to direct plays, *and* to act as Artistic Director of an off-off-Broadway theater called Theatre-Off-Park. As if this weren't enough, my courses at Hunter included a playwriting seminar, where I studied writing for the first and only time, and for which I wrote two full-length plays. One was an adaptation of a classic Gothic novel, Matthew Lewis's *The Monk*. Turning a four-hundred-and-twenty page, multi-character, triple-plotted novel set during the Spanish Inquisition into a two-act play with a small cast was a challenge, to say the least, but one that taught me a great deal about writing—and one that preceded directly the writing of *Bunnicula*.

The idea for the *character* of Bunnicula was mine, but the idea of turning the character into a *book* was Debbie's mother's. I honestly don't remember where the character came from, but my guess is that my almost instinctive sense of parody was inspired by all those late-night vampire movies—with perhaps a little help from the Marx Brothers and a dash of seasoning from Sherlock Holmes and his colleague, Dr. John Watson, who

My birthday-card drawing of Bunnicula.

would ultimately and unconsciously serve as models for the detective team of Chester the cat and Harold the dog.

But I am getting ahead of myself.

In the beginning, there was only Bunnicula; and he was nothing more than a free-floating character in my head who, on one occasion, served as material for a homemade birthday card. At some point, Debbie told her mother about him.

"A vampire rabbit," her mother said. "What a wonderful character for a children's book. The two of you love to write. Why don't you try it?"

"Sounds like fun," was my response when Debbie told me that night of their conversation. And so we cleared the dinner dishes from the tomato-red table in the kitchen, and put words on paper for the first time.

We knew next to nothing about children's books, had never heard of Judy Blume or Beverly Cleary, couldn't have told you what was meant by a "middle-grade novel." If there was any model for our writing, it was—for me, at least—*Charlotte's Web*. Debbie's models were more likely Bram Stoker, Jane Austen, and Mary Shelley. But I doubt either of us was aware of models. What we set out to do was write a story to entertain ourselves, not imitate someone else's style or figure out what we were supposed to do when writing for children. We gave little thought to being published, none at all to establishing careers as children's book authors.

That first scrap of paper held all the main ingredients of the book save one. There's no mention of Harold, only Bunnicula's "war with household cat, Chester." But Chester's means of foiling Bunnicula—and therefore most of the plot of the book—are listed in neat numerical order and are all based on legendary methods of destroying or defending oneself from vampires: garlic, immersion in water, driving a stake (steak) through the heart. The only one we left out was the use of a crucifix to repel vampires. We may not have known much about writing for children, but our instincts told us that the inclusion of a crucifix in a tale about a vampire bunny was, at best, in questionable taste.

Whether we discussed Harold or not that night, I don't recall. All I know is that when I returned from work late the next afternoon, Debbie had written the beginning of the story—and there on the page was Harold come to life, with his tired old eyes and distinctive voice.

From that evening on, our working method remained much the same. We settled into a comfortable place to work, most often at either end of the living room sofa, and talked the story through. Using a pad of lined white paper, soon to be replaced by a three-ring notebook of yellow lined paper, we took turns recording the words that flew so quickly out of our mouths. It wasn't easy for whoever was writing to keep up, but how easy I remember it being to spin that story from our imaginations. We wrote no character histories, did none of the kind of prewriting I so often do now for my novels, just put a few notes down on a single sheet of paper and began to play. Looking at that first handwritten version of *Bunnicula*, I can spot something I *know* was Debbie's (the Roumanian sheet music) or mine (Chester's kitty sweater with the sixteen purple mice), but more often than not, I

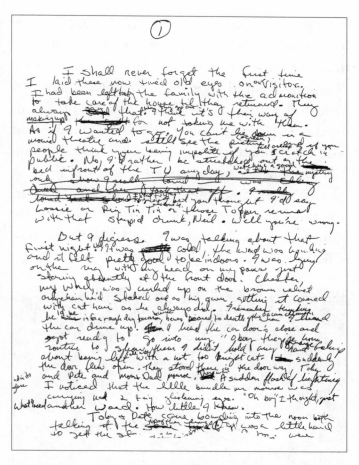

don't know who was responsible for what. There were many times that one of us began a sentence and the other finished it.

Most of the first draft of the book reflects the final version. There were very few substantial changes. Toby started out being the older, more obnoxious brother; Pete, the younger, smarter one. By the next draft, they had changed places. Similarly, Harold started out, at least in the first half of the first draft, being the smarter of the animal team. He even refers to Chester at one point as "a not-too-bright cat," an observation borne out by Chester's apparently not knowing what glass is when describing the grandfather clock in the third chapter. Referring to the swinging pendulum as a toy he wanted to play with, we had Chester say:

Moose, foreground, with Gudrun peeking over his shoulder, in the living room of the garret apartment in Brooklyn Heights where *Bunnicula* was begun. Much of the first draft was written on the sofa at the right.

"I couldn't even get to the toy. Somebody had put this hard, slippery stuff in front of it. You know, like the stuff they put in windows and TV sets. It's dangerous."

"Glass."

"That's it."

Well, with two cats and no dogs in the family, we couldn't keep Chester *that* dumb. Besides, we really did believe that cats were smarter than dogs— or at least that they made more of a pretense of it— and so felt compelled to restore what we saw as a natural order. In the final version of *Bunnicula*, Chester knows what glass is, but does retain a bit of his former obtuseness in not being observant or knowledgeable enough to know that there *is* in fact glass in a grandfather clock.

Although we never wrote him as such, we at first envisioned Bunnicula to be a different sort of character from the one who evolved—one who spoke, for starters—and one who was much more a traditional vampire, malevolent and bloodthirsty. Had we drawn him as we had first conceived him, Chester's suspicions would have been entirely justified! But the idea of a little bunny rabbit leaping great heights to sink his fangs into his human victims' necks seemed just a little too far-fetched, even for us. Besides, logic told us that if there were such a thing as a vampire rabbit, he would most likely be a vegetarian. And so Bunnicula's victims became carrots and tomatoes and, in one of my favorite scenes in the book, a poor, unsuspecting zucchini!

The reason for making Bunnicula mute was simple: It allowed him to remain much more of a mystery.

Writing the book became part of the fabric of our lives, but only one thread among many, and not a major thread at that. Some days we wrote for an hour, some for fifteen minutes. Many days we didn't write at all. I was occupied with the demands of my work and studies and trying to run a theater and direct plays on the side. If not exactly occupied, Debbie found herself more and more distracted by the pain she was experiencing in her lower back.

The pain grew worse over a period of months, and by the late spring of 1977, it was beginning to make it hard for her to get around. No doctor seemed able to diagnose the problem. As much as it was becoming more of an inconvenience and obstacle in everyday life, Debbie's biggest concern was that the problem—whatever it was—would mean we would have to cancel our planned trip to England in

August. Neither of us had ever traveled outside our own country, and Debbie, who had read volumes of English history and was a passionate Anglophile, could barely wait to set foot on British soil.

She had always said one of the reasons she wanted to be an actress was so that she could wear costumes of other times and places and transport herself back, become a piece of history, feel it come alive around her. She wrote in a journal once, "I believe that heaven is nothing more than a movie of the whole history of the world that you may watch at your leisure." It was her idea of heaven, anyway, and the prospect of *being* on those streets in England, inside the walls of those castles and inns and cathedrals, walking through the landscape that was the stage of the history that so fascinated her—this must surely have been her idea of heaven on earth.

We were scheduled to leave on the twenty-second of August.

A little less than a month earlier, on the twenty-seventh of July, in the middle of the night, Debbie was rushed by ambulance from our apartment in Brooklyn to St. Vincent's Hospital in Manhattan, her back pain so severe she couldn't stand or walk.

It was four in the morning. I sat alone in the emergency waiting room, writing a letter to my parents on small pieces of note paper given to me by the receptionist on duty. I don't remember what I wrote them, except for one thing. I told them I accepted the inevitability that as much as we wanted them, Debbie and I would never have children. Even then, I suspect I knew what I was doing. I was bargaining with God.

We did not go to England. On August eleventh, one day before her thirty-first birthday, we learned that Debbie had cancer and that it was terminal. The recurring benign cyst in her upper jaw (called an ameloblastoma) had turned malignant and spread throughout her body. This occurrence was described in more than one medical report as "extremely rare."

Debbie remained in the hospital for almost two months. In late September, she moved into her parents' apartment in the Riverdale section of the Bronx, the apartment where she had lived from the age of twelve until she had gone off to college. A hospital bed was moved into her old bedroom, and after a time of shuttling back and forth between Brooklyn where I lived and Manhattan where I worked and the Bronx where my heart was,

I found someone to live in our apartment and take care of Gudrun and Moose, and I, too, moved into my in-laws' home.

Even in the hardest of times, the sun rises and the sun sets and we are hungry and must eat and we brush our teeth and we wash our clothes and we read the morning paper. And it is the very ordinariness of life that makes it all so surreal. And soon we find ourselves doing things we would have once said were surreal, and they become ordinary, and there are no longer any distinctions between the two, and that is when the days become one long day.

For ten months, I spoke to doctors and nurses every day on the phone or in person. Every day, I filled pieces of paper with lists of questions and hastily scribbled notations about symptoms and treatments and pain medications. I started each day crying in the shower and then I dried my tears along with the rest of me and went to work and came home from work and ate my dinner and watched TV with Debbie in the evening and slept in the twin bed next to her hospital bed and worried and had bad dreams and went on.

Debbie, too, went on, neither a hero nor a martyr, but a person afflicted with illness trying to live each moment as it comes. She would return to the hospital four more times over the next eight months, spending nearly as much time there as she did in her parents' home.

Early on, she confided in me her fear that she would not, in her words, be good at dying. She worried that she would disappoint others by failing to live up to the images of the brave and beautiful people who died of mysterious and often unnamed illnesses every night in television dramas or in the movies. But she didn't take into account that her beauty was natural and more than skin deep, and that she had had a lifetime of learning to be brave. And so, when friends and family members came to visit, which they did nearly every day, she smiled through her pain, and when asked how she was doing, most often replied, "Oh, tell me what's going on in *your* life. It's so much more interesting."

At some point that fall, I typed up the six chapters we had written and, when Debbie was feeling up to it, we returned to telling each other the story of Bunnicula, the vampire rabbit. I can't place the moment, where it happened or when; in truth, I have no memory at all of writing the book from that time on. I trust that some of it was written in the hospital, some in the apartment in Riverdale.

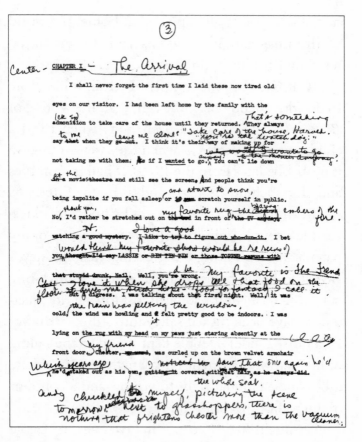

But I can't see us in my mind's eye, can't connect the words on the page to the hands that wrote them. The only connection I can make is to the sound of laughter. That I can hear. Cleansing laughter, washing away the taint of sickness and dread, releasing us to that blessed place where we had always been so happy and at home: the world of the imagination, of words and dreams unfettered by hard-hearted reality.

Wait. There *is* one moment I recall. It has more to do with a teddy bear, though, than the writing of *Bunnicula*. The bear had been mine when I was a child, my older brothers' when they were young, so it probably dates from the 1930s. It had button eyes and slots behind its head and arms for fingers to slip in and animate its worn, nubby body. I had rescued it a couple of years earlier from the attic of my parents' home; during Debbie's first hospital stay, I gave it to her to be her mascot. After a scare during which we thought it had been lost forever (it turned out to have been tucked safely into a dresser drawer by a nurse's aide), Debbie kept it tied to the railing of her bed with a bright pink length of yarn, where it became a familiar sight to visitors and a constant friend to both Debbie and me.

I brought Teddy to life many times, to cajole Debbie out of her sadness and make her laugh, to turn bad moments on their heads, to give us both the freedom we needed to escape. It wasn't long before Teddy took on a clear, strong, and surprisingly aggressive personality. "Pay attention to me" seemed to be his credo.

At one point in the writing of *Bunnicula*, he demanded to know when we were going to write *his* story. "I've had a fascinating life, you know," he told us. "Your readers would be far more interested in my adventures than those of a silly old vampire rabbit!"

The only way to quiet him down was to promise to write his story. Which we did, of course, not wanting to put up with the nattering of a cranky, egotistical teddy bear any more than we had to. But then, how smart he was to know we needed something to look forward to as we approached the end of writing *Bunnicula*.

By the time Debbie died on June 3, 1978, she was the coauthor of two children's books: *Bunnicula, A Rabbit-Tale of Mystery* and *Teddy Bear's Scrapbook*. She had also written a book of her own. Called *Petey the Parakeet*, it lovingly and humorously recalled her one childhood pet. The book was bought for publication, but, unfortunately, never published.

Debbie also came up with an invention during this time for a picture frame that would allow a roll of developed film to be stored inside so that the image could be changed at one's whim. I did a patent search for this invention, while a close friend

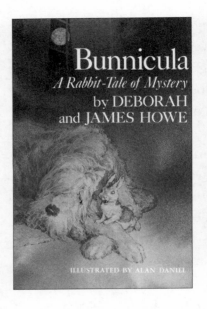

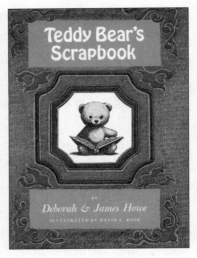

who was a furniture-maker and antique-restorer made a prototype. Nothing came of it ultimately, but I see now how important it was to Debbie to leave something of herself behind. A book of her own. An invention. Something, something to let the world know she had been there.

She did leave something behind, of course. To those who knew her, she left warmth and light to help us through whatever dark nights we had yet to endure without her there beside us. One of the nurses who took care of her said to me once, "When I go into most patients' rooms, it's strictly routine. But when I go into Debbie's room, it's as if it was lit by a thousand candles."

To those who would never know her, she left Harold and Chester, a piece of Roumanian sheet music, words and laughter; she left her name on the cover of a book that has only grown in popularity over the twenty years since its publication and is now being read by its first readers to children of their own.

My father often wrote in a circular style, coming back at the end to where he had begun. It is a style I often use myself. And so I return to my first sentence—

What happened I do not remember now.

The words are not mine. I took them whole from a short story by Guy de Maupassant called "Was it a Dream?" When I read them, I thought how perfectly they described the failure of memory, especially when one is recalling a time in one's life that is filled with emergencies and unexpected twists and sorrow. A time, even while it's lived, that is a blur.

But as *Bunnicula* celebrates the twentieth anniversary of its publication, it is a time for looking back and remembering, and I found I did remember, not all of the details, but a tomato-red table and a coffee-stained scrap of paper; the sound of laughter; and the good company of words—words, with their power to create characters and worlds, to light up the darkness and, in the face of impossibility, make anything seem possible.

–J.H.
Hastings-on-Hudson, NY
April 18, 1999